Forbidden Love

Julie Griffin Pritchard

A BBTS Publication
Deri, Bargoed.
BBTS (Baarbaara The Sheep Publications)
Est. Feb 2012
email: **baarbaarathesheep@hotmail.co.uk**
baarbaarathesheep/wordpress.com

Baarbaara
The Sheep

ISBN-13: 9798506505686

Imprint: Independently published

KDP Assigned ISBN registered with Booksinprint.com

Images © Julie Griffin Pritchard
Typeset: Times New Roman/Gabriola

About the Author:

Julie Pritchard nee Griffin was born in Cardiff and grew up in Ely, she later moved to the beautiful Rhymney Valley. Julie is a published performance poet and author of 'Butterfly Kisses and a Bee Sting Mind' 'Healing Garden' 'Spirit Cracked not Broken' and 'Between Aurora and Twilight' 'Forbidden Love' is Julie's first novel.

www.pritchardjulie5wordpress.com

Writing 'Forbidden Love'

It has taken me 8 years to write 'Forbidden Love' Many rejections and bad advice, so I decided to self publish. In 2012 all I had to go on was self belief and my love for Ireland and my grandmother. All I knew about Nana's Irish family, was her two brothers, Alec and Christy, and the story of Kevin Barry. Then, Joseph Knox, Chrissie's grandson, made contact from Dublin. He devised a wonderful family tree. From this I found James, Chrissie, Essie, Mary Josephine and many more of my Irish relatives.

He travelled from Dublin to Cardiff with his brother Bernard to meet with me and other members of my family. When I met with my two Irish cousins they were astounded how much I looked like their grandmother Christina (Chrissie) and when I visited them in Dublin their sister said the same.

How strange I had a job at Jacobs Biscuit factory like Chrissie but I turned it down. I chose to work in a sewing factory like Nana. I also took part in many demonstrations, like Chrissie and Maggie. 'The Right to Work' March, shouting "out, Maggie, out, out, out," the Miners' Strike, Greenham Common Marches, the 'Stop the War Coalition.' I marched against the invasion of Iraq and resigned as a councillor over the invasion, I also marched for Syria.

In 2014, I visited Christy's son, Christopher, in Limerick.
Chris gave me the layout of Red Cow Lane, O'Donovan
Rossa and the story of my father looking like Elvis. Sadly,
Chris Crosbie died in 2016.

I also visited Kilmainham Gaol and wept where they shot the
Sixteen. I walked the streets Nana walked, played and lived.

In 2015, I walked the coast of Donegal and Antrim. I was
flying home from Dublin. The night before I flew home to
Wales, I called in to 'Cobblestones' that was once called
'Carolans'. The pub was opposite where Nana lived. I read
and performed my poetry, the same place my father sang in
1957 and where my Nana and her family drank. I had many
drinks bought for me that night. Irish, Brazilian, Germans,
Americans and Spanish. I declined most of the drinks
because I was flying home early in the morning.

At the end of the evening and after many goodbyes I
walked outside Cobblestones, looked up to the summer clear
sky and I knew my father and my Irish relatives were looking
down.

Nana never spoke of what she witnessed, only Kevin Barry. I
believe that Nana was too traumatised. Dublin from 1916 to

when Nana left 1921 was equivalent to Syria and Iraq. War torn and broken. I took up the pen and chose to write what Nana could not talk about.

Review by poet, Ceri Creffield

Two families in two cities, two young people who will bring division and discord to those they love. Julie Pritchard's story of ill-fated lovers unfolds like a screenplay against a backdrop of some of the most significant events in Irish and British history.

In Dublin, the Caffreys struggle to overcome desperate poverty and personal tragedy, caught up in the struggle for Irish independence and the turbulent events of the early twentieth century.

In Cardiff Richard Griffin grows up in a poor and unhappy household until he is conscripted into the British Army to fight in the Great War. Posted later to Dublin, he is drawn to Maggie Caffrey, youngest daughter of her family.

Forbidden Love charts the battles the young couple must fight to be together and the fractured relationships that ensue. It evokes the harsh realities of poverty, the prejudice and hatred engendered by sectarianism and the difficult choices faced by those with divided loyalties. The personal and the political are in constant proximity but not always in agreement and a price must be paid for both. The complex narrative is at once a love story and an examination of the conflict between different beliefs and ideals and the lengths to which people may be driven to defend them.

Review by poet and novelist, Alan Roderick

Julie Pritchard's *Forbidden Love* is a 'family saga' with a difference. Far from being creations of her own imagination, the main protagonists are all members of her own family, in particular her grandparents, Maggie and Dick, whose love story this novel celebrates. Maggie Caffery grows up in Dublin whilst Dick Griffin is born and brought up in Cardiff. Ordinarily, they might never have met but a chain of circumstances brings them together. Maggie Caffery is part of a strongly Republican Dublin family and, at first, wants nothing to do with the shy advances of the British soldier on guard duty outside the Leinster Sewing Factory where she works.

It is an encounter which will change both their lives as slowly, but surely, they fall in love. Dick is willing to give up home and family to start a new life together with Maggie in Ireland, but that is never an option, as public opinion and, in particular, the IRA would never stand for such a liaison.

Julie is a performance poet (and there is a poetic intensity about the best bits of *Forbidden Love)* and has published several volumes of poetry. *Forbidden Love* is her first novel. She makes no secret of where her sympathies lie in the struggle for supremacy in Ireland and it is the dramatic scenes set in Ireland which will live longest in the memory of this reviewer.

Julie Pritchard (née Julie Griffin) has done, not just her own family, but the rest of us, a favour, in bringing her grandparent's love story, with its Romeo and Juliet overtones, a Celtic connection, if ever there was one, to a wider audience.

Celtic Heart

I feel you through my veins.

My heart is sore over the loss of what was.

Is my Celtic soul from all of what you were?

Have I risen from your poverty, fear and shame?

Can I belong, turn around, go back and change.

Or must I stay in limbo, read of what was,

listen to what others say.

Do I need atonement from others for the mistakes

that were made of forbidden fruit?

Must I look to the truth and find that love conquers all.

Julie Pritchard nee Griffin 2012

The poem Celtic Heart is in my first collection titled
'Butterfly Kisses and a Bee Sting Mind'

"Did I tell you about Kevin Barry?" A tear would fall and I caught her memories and gave them life.

Prologue

The door was opened and there in the golden sun rays her silver hair shone, her glasses were like jam jars' bottoms and the smell of bleach and cabbage wafted towards me. She spoke with a light Irish accent "Ah who is it?" and I would reply "Julie, Nana." "Don't tell me which Julie let me feel your face." Her warm hands cupped my face and she would say, "Ah, it is Francis's Julie, come in." I followed Nana down the narrow passage, following the round plum shape that swayed from side to side, wearing a tie up the back wrap around floral pinny and on her feet were soft comfortable slippers. Nana swayed into the small kitchen, I to the square lounge, where I sat on the pale grey PVC two seater sofa.

Sat opposite me was my Grandfather who we called Grampy Dick. He never said much, he sat in his chair and grinned, he dressed smartly at all times and always wore a tie. He was very fair skinned with rheumy light blue eyes, he had a pale mole on his left eye lid that would move up and down when he smiled. His mop of auburn hair had gone with age and now a bare head shone. He let out a cough and asked after the family. Before I could answer Nana would say in a tongue and cheek way, "Ah shut up, Dick, no one is talking to you."

She carried on chatting to me from the kitchen, then swayed in carrying a tray with chocolate biscuits and a glass of warm lemonade. I looked up to her face, her once deep blue eyes were now milky blue due to the diabetes, she had facial hair above her lip. Her eyes and upper lip mesmerised me. I thanked her for my drink. The warm sweet lemonade slid down my throat and the half chocolate biscuit melted on my hand. I felt anxious about the sticky chocolate which had spread to the middle of my palm. I stared at the chocolate stain and wished it would go away. She sat beside me smelling of lavender soap and then she held my hand, yes the chocolate stained hand. "What am I like, I should have given you a tissue." She slapped her broad lap and giggled. I noticed the thin gold wedding ring, worn away by the many years my grandparents were married.

My eyes travelled around the room, to the photo of Nana when she was younger. A black and white photo surrounded by a glass like mirror frame. Her hair was styled in a short bob, her smile radiated out of the photo, she looked beautiful. Next to the television was a metal grey, talking tape machine, her talking books were stacked to the side. A glass cabinet full of treasured ornaments, bought by family members over the years. The blue and white statue of the

Blessed Virgin Mary sat in the middle of the beech wood veneer sideboard. It was full of holy water from my younger brother Sean's last trip to Lourdes. On top of the television sat family photos encased in their frames. There was a school photo of my eldest brother and I looking like a pair of albinos, very light skinned, white blond hair and pale eyes. I gazed at the black velvet antimacassars, they reminded me of cockney pearly Kings' and Queens' hats close up. From a distance they were sequins that had been embroidered on to velvet and depicted old scenes of Dublin. A constant reminder of what she gave up and left behind. She placed her hands on her lap cleared her throat and say "Ah did I tell you about Kevin Barry?" Then a tear would fall down her lined cheek.

Part One

DUBLIN

1899 - 1920

In Ireland 1899, Queen Victoria was on the throne and Lord Salisbury was prime minister. Dublin was the Capital of Britain's first colony and the second biggest City in the Empire. Dublin was known as the City of Saints and Scholars. However, Ireland was in a bitter state of unrest. Horrific deaths due to the potato famine. The fear of starvation was filled with Catholicism and this instilled even more fear. Many left Ireland. Those left behind lived under the adoption of the laissez- faire policy in nineteen century England.

The Government often concealed an admission that a problem was insoluble or that it must be endured because nobody could think of a method of solving it! Ireland's crisis was allowed to develop because no English party saw a solution in the generation after the Napoleonic wars. The Country's resources were not improved to keep pace in production. The horrific treatment of Fenian political prisoners and also the rape of their language and Celtic culture. Low wages, poor working conditions. High rents, corrupt landlords and the poverty.

There were many failed uprisings. However, all the above festered into a wound that grew in the young! The boil was ready for bursting, to be lanced by the rise of republicanism!

Kavanagh's Court was one of many Georgian buildings that were left by the wealthy, now in the hands of the Dublin Corporation and corrupt business men. Kavanagh's Court sat in the pea soup, sulphurous coal flavoured fug. The Georgian tenement blocks were infested with filth and where fifty families lived cheek by jowl, sharing one tap and toilet.

Kavanagh's Court looked over the whole of Dublin Town, General Post Office, the old library, Trinity College Dublin, The Four Courts, the river Liffey snaking its way through and in the distance the spire of St Patrick's Cathedral. In the middle stood the tall brick chimney of Jameson's distillery. The area was known as Smithfield. And at the centre of Smithfield was a busy bustling market that sold livestock, fruit, vegetables and fish. The air was filled with food smells, Jeyes fluid, lavender from the lavender seller, the oak aroma of Jameson's distillery smoking its various malted grains, sulphurous coal and the stench of Dublin Docks.

It was the end of January 1899. Mary Caffery looked out of the spotlessly cleaned sash window. Margaret, known as Maggie, was 3 weeks old, suckled at her mother's breast. Mary stared beyond the soot filled fog. The stench of stale urine and shit from the other tenants was making its way from the gap under the door. Mary never got used to that

3

familiar malodorous stink. Her husband Patrick sailed past on his cart ready for his daily rounds. Patrick was following his mother, Esther. Esther was a self employed Master Carter. She rented stables at Red Cow lane. Patrick carted coal, barley, sometimes furniture through the busy city of Dublin. Patrick worked alongside his mother Esther. Esther was a tall thin woman with jet black hair tied in a neat bun. However, despite her strength and feistiness, she, like most Irish women, accepted her husband Alexander's gambling and drinking.

The room was large and split in two by red velvet curtains that had seen better days. On the other side of the curtain, and sleeping on one mattress, were her three children, James, Christina known as Chrissie and Esther known as Essie. The bare wooden floor boards were scrubbed clean. The fire in the black leaded fireplace crackled and spat. On the other side of the room was a table and four chairs and pans used for cooking on an open fire. To the right were two zinc buckets, the buckets served as a sink and toilet.

In the corner was a deep red elegant chaise lounge, that looked out of place. Mary treasured the chaise lounge. It was given to her from her former employer. A door led to Mary and Patrick's small bedroom, an old metal frame bed

filled the tiny room and this was where Maggie slept.
Mary wiped her face with the back of her hand and
swallowed her bitter tears grabbed her white rosary beads
and prayed for a better home.

The Caffery family added more children to their
family. Two boys, Alexander known as Alec and Christy.
Mary and Patrick's eldest child James was diagnosed with
epilepsy. Irish society thought it was best to hide people like
James away.

It was a mild spring morning when the authorities
came and Mary had no intentions of letting them in. Father
Flynn quietly told Mary that she would be arrested and that
would leave her children without their mother. Mary
screamed, "I can look after him. He is my boy." Patrick
stared helplessly. Chrissie and Essie sobbed and held onto
their mother. James, bewildered, shed silent tears.

Maggie and her two brothers played outside in the
poverty stricken streets. James, aged thirteen, was taken from
the arms of his loving family and became a patient at
Grangegorman's hospital for the insane. Mary fell onto the
floor with her two daughters in an emotional heap. Father
Flynn spoke again and said, "It is for the best Mrs Caffery."
Chrissie stared hard at the priest, her green eyes full of
hatred.

Maggie grew into a rebellious child, she often ran through the market nicking an apple along the way and leaving her laughter behind. Her two older sisters, Chrissie and Essie, were too sophisticated. She preferred her two younger brothers' company, climbing trees at St Stephan's Green. Always scabby kneed and tide mark necked and wiping her nose in her sleeve. More than anything Maggie wanted to be a boy!

In late autumn of 1909, Mary's prayers were answered. The family were moving from poverty, and the toilet they shared with 50 other families, to a better home. Up the road to where Patrick and his mother kept their horses. Number 1, Red Cow Lane. The property was a detached house and had two rooms downstairs, one was a mean kitchen cum scullery and a backroom, upstairs were two bedrooms. The property was surrounded by a brick wall and a tall wooden gate with a smaller gate for easy access. There was a large yard with an outside toilet, outbuildings, stables and a haystack. Opposite was the pub Carolans, where Alexander Caffery spent his time.

Maggie and her brothers ran round the yard dancing and giggling, while their parents unloaded the furniture. Mary and Patrick stopped for a breather, Mary, hands on her broad hips, Patrick wiped his brow. Both stood in the middle of the hay strewn yard and stared at each other. He smiled, he could see happiness in his wife's pale green eyes, he took advantage of this and squeezed her hand in affection. She withdrew her hand. Mary had no time for affection. Off she bustled into her new home, rolled up her sleeves and began to dish out orders to her giggling children. While Patrick spoke to his favourite horse called Ned.

A cold January 1910, the wind whipped off the Irish Sea and on to the city of Dublin, sleet swirled in the air. Patrick, a short thin man, was home early from his round. He whispered to his wife, "Mary I have a stinking headache and feel sick." Mary, a buxom woman, with fine white hair that was styled into a bun, was aware that for a while Patrick had been complaining of a headache and she noticed he looked pale. Mary kindly chastised her husband by telling him to keep his cap on when he was on his rounds.

Like most working class families, they could not afford a doctor so they visited the chemist, Mr Mayer. Mr Mayer had a shop off North King Street. He knew most things and had potions for everything. "Look here, Patrick, I will visit Mr Mayer and see what he says, have a little nap while the house is quiet, I will not be long." She put her coat

7

on and wrapped a shawl around her head. The icy wind made her eyes water, so she bent her head and walked towards the chemist. She turned the old wooden door knob and was greeted by warmth, a healthy clean herb smell, and a collection of coloured bottles, lotions, potions and pills that were packed into glass fronted cabinets. Behind the small counter stood Mr Mayer, a short man with a dark moustache and hair slicked back, wearing little round silver spectacles. "Morning to you, Mrs Caffery, what can I do for you?"

"Mr Mayer, it is himself, he has had this headache for a while."

"What part of the head?"

Mary put her hand to her head and had to think. "I am not sure, he just said he has a headache."

"Ah, this cold weather could be affecting his sinuses. Look, I will give you some eucalyptus oil. Tell him to put it in hot water and breathe in the mixture."

"God bless you, Mr Mayer, how much do I owe you?"

"A penny."

Mary paid the chemist. "Grand, that is grand. Good day to you Mr Mayer."

Outside the streets busied and bustled, her thoughts went towards the evening meal and how Patrick being home had interfered with her cooking preparations. The bitter wind knifed through her and she was glad the pea soup mist had lifted taking the stench of sulphur and coal away and replacing it with clear sea air. Her frozen hands struggled to open the door, once inside the door slammed shut. She took off her scarf and coat and rubbed herself down. She saw Patrick slumped forward, head down on the kitchen table. She quietly chastised him but there was no response. Her rough callous hands touched his shoulder and she realised she had not touched him in years. She then noticed blood from his ear and mouth. Her mind raced along to tell her heart it will be broken any minute. She called his name out loud, "Patrick!" and shook him again and shouted, "You cannot leave me now. God not now!" She fell to her knees and cradled him like a child and howled like an animal.

Outside in the yard was Esther, Patrick's mother. She stopped when she heard her daughter-in-law's cries. She clutched the reins, she knew something was terribly wrong, her body shook as she guided the horse and cart through the gates. She stumbled across the yard, opened the back door and felt a sensation that made her hair stand on end. Esther took a deep breath as her heart boomed in her chest. As she entered she saw Mary holding her only son. Mary looked up, her face was distorted in grief. "Mammy he's gone from me, he's gone."

Esther slipped onto the floor, both women were lost in grief, their tears mingled with each other's and fell onto Patrick's face. Mary in her insanity thought a doctor was needed to save Patrick. She turned her back on her husband who was being cradled by his mother. She opened the back door and stumbled to her neighbour Mrs Kenny. Mrs Kenny, a tiny woman with a mop of red hair that never looked tidy. Holding her sixth child on her hip, she opened the door and could see by Mary's face something terrible had happened. "Mrs Kenny can you go to the Dublin Union and please get a doctor for me, it's Patrick…." She stopped in mid sentence.

Mary fell towards her home, her shoulders moved in unison with her sobs. She opened the gate, walked past Esther's horse and cart, heard Patrick's horse braying from the stable door. She glanced and turned away and fell to her knees onto the frozen yard, the smell of horse manure filled her nostrils. She felt the sting of bile and tea at the back of her throat, she ran to the outside toilet and vomited. She wiped her mouth and realised she was not wearing a coat.

She opened the door and saw her mother-in-law laying her beloved husband out on the floor, covering Patrick with a sheet. Esther looked up nervously, brushed her hands over her dress, then her hair and said, "We need a priest to

10

give the last rites." Mary did not hear her mother-in-law. She knelt by her dead husband, wiped his ashen grey face with her hankie. Esther knelt next to her daughter-in-law and both wailed.

Suddenly Mrs Kenny walked in. "Mrs Caffery, I spoke to the landlord at Carolans, he's gone to the hospital for you." Mary and Esther continued praying, Mrs Kenny's eyes rested on Patrick Caffery. She made a sign of the cross and offered her condolences. Then Mrs Kenny interrupted the grief stricken women's prayers. "Mrs Caffery, I normally help out with the laying of the dead..." Mary's tear stained face looked at Mrs Kenny, "Thank you for getting the doctor for me, but me and my mother-in-law will..." Mary stopped talking, the pain in her heart reminded her that Patrick was dead and that she would never see him again. "Mrs Caffery, I understand," said Mrs Kenny, "I will leave you now with your grief."

A gentle tapping stopped Mary from wailing again. It was Doctor O'Sullivan. The kind faced, short stocky doctor, who dressed in tweed no matter what season, quietly spoke, "What has happened to your husband, Mrs Caffery?" Mary gulped down a sob and pointed to the floor to where Patrick was lying. The Doctor knelt down and noticed there was blood coming from the patient's ears. He knew this was

11

a brain injury. "Mrs Caffery, has your husband had a knock recently or had he been complaining of any headaches?"

Mary found her composure and answered the doctor, "Yes, doctor, for the past couple of days, we thought he had a head cold."

"I am sorry Mrs Caffery, we will have to take your husband to the hospital and find out the cause of death."

Mary cried "Oh no, last rites! I need a priest!"

Esther, in her madness, ran past her horse and cart and ran to St Paul's church on Arran Quay to fetch Father Flynn. She did not want her only son going to purgatory and linger in limbo between this world and the next. She found the priest coming out of the church and begged him to come quickly. The priest buttoned up his coat and hurriedly followed Esther, breathlessly they arrived at Red Cow Lane.

Essie, Maggie, Alec and Christie arrived home from school and sensed something was wrong when they noticed the curtains were closed. and Granny Caffery was in the kitchen eyes red rimmed. Esther looked at the bewildered faces of her four young grandchildren, blew her nose and said, "Come, sit – sit. Yer dada's gone to heaven and is with the angels and saints."

Maggie cried out, "Daddy my daddy."

Essie, sensitive by nature, wiped her tears with her embroidered hankie and softly said, "Where is Mammy?" Her Granny coughed, "Your mammy has gone to the hospital to stay with your Da."

The two younger brothers felt sad and uneasy and went outside to the stables, followed by Maggie. Through tears and sobs they told their father's favourite horse, Ned, about his master's death. Chrissie arrived home from work to an outpouring of sobs and cries. Her Granny held her hand and told Chrissie. Chrissie looked at the floor, tears streamed down her beautiful pale face and for once she was lost for words.

Patrick died at the age of forty-four from a Cerebral Haemorrhage. Mary aged fifty-four was a widow with six children. Patrick's sudden unexpected death devastated the family. Mary, a proud woman, was full of anguish because she did not have enough money to bury her husband. Patrick was the main bread winner. She had money from Chrissie who worked at 'Jacobs' but this was not enough. She broke down in front of her mother-in-law. "Mammy, what am I going to do? I did not expect Patrick to die. I have money but not enough for a funeral."

Esther took Mary's hand. "Mary child, do not worry.

I have money put aside. I will pay for the funeral. He was, after all, my only son."

Three days later, the Caffery family prepared Patrick's wake. Patrick lay in the open coffin wearing a white shroud, entwined in his hands was a blue rosary. A lit candle gave light to the room that smelled of polished wood, candle wax and a hint of whiskey. Prayers, sobbing and cries filled the sad air.

The day of Patrick's funeral was a cold bone-biting day. Mary, distraught, was with her father and mother-in-law. Behind were Chrissie and Essie, holding hands with their younger siblings, following the coffin. Many family members, Patrick's sister Sarah and her husband James Boyce, were there as well. Patrick's other sister, Josephine Mary, was also there with her sometimes husband Denis. Esther made sure Josephine Mary was dressed accordingly and that she was reasonably sober.

Mary's brother, Joseph Murray, was there to show support for his older sister. They all made their way to mass and to say their goodbyes. Alexander, Patrick's father and other men went to Glasnevin cemetery to bury his only son. Afterwards the men came back to Red Cow Lane. All gathered telling stories, songs were sung and drink flowed. Mary looked at her wedding ring and twisted the tarnished ring around her finger, she stopped and reflected back to her parents, James and Margaret Murray. They came from a little village twenty miles outside Dublin, called St Margaret's. The area was known to have had a Fairy Fort and was once a pagan site and the locals thought that fairies really lived there. Her parents ran away and eloped to the big city of Dublin for a better life. Sadly they did not find a better life in Dublin and were too ashamed to go back to St Margaret's. They now lived with many others in squalor and poverty and James struggled to find reliable work.

Mary was their first born. Mary witnessed the loss of her mother's six children whose ages ranged from three months to two years. Mary's mother in her frailty began to rely on her for most things and Mary became the mother. She witnessed her mother's grief and mental misery that went with the pain of the early deaths. She remembered the words her mother said to the fragile baby lying at her breast. "Come on, little one, she is not suckling and she feels so cold." Mary would take the baby from her mother's thin arms. Then her mother would wrap the ragged shawl around her bone thin shoulders. Silently, Mary shut the door, and once outside in the filthy decaying communal hallway, she leaned against the door waiting for reality to hit her mother. The scream of grief and insanity bounced off the walls.

Mary breathed in deep, held her breath and ran to the local midwife and funeral director. Mary was ten when the last of her siblings died. However, a brother survived named Joseph. The responsibility of looking after her mother and the sadness of the early deaths scarred Mary and she decided from an early age not to marry.

Her memories took her back to where she met Patrick. Patrick said he noticed her at her place of work and it was her platinum blond hair and her eyes of pale green. Patrick's hair was raven black and his complexion was old Irish, very dark. He was twenty six, she was thirty six.

She recalled the house where she worked as a housekeeper for an English family. Mary did not live in, she chose to stay at home because of her mother's illness. The Ackerman family ran a retail business and owned property. She was not keen on her boss, Mr Ackerman. Mr Ackerman never spoke to Mary only at her. His wife, Mrs Ackerman was different, a tall elegant woman with a warm compassionate personality.

Mr Ackerman came from London and moved over to Ireland with his wife Jemima. Jemima Laverson's family was wealthy, very wealthy and the marriage was not one of love, it was an arranged marriage, a marriage of convenience. Mr Ackerman was Jewish and a conceited and arrogant man. Mary often wondered how her employer was mean minded, and lacked any care for the Jews who came from Russia and Poland, fleeing the terrifying pogroms and hoping to find a better life in Ireland. These poor starving refugees sometimes could not afford the rent from the Ackerman's property and some were thrown onto the streets.

Mary's mind wandered to number 10, Dominick Street. The door was painted ruby red with a brass door handle that you could see your face in. Mary cleaned and rubbed the door knocker as if her life depended on it. She cleaned it at 10am every Thursday. At the same time Patrick would be passing with his horse and cart on his delivery round. Patrick would drive past, look and wave, Mary never responded. Patrick noticed her blushed cheeks, he liked to think it was him, no, it was the hard work and the elbow grease.

Mary was a conscientious worker, diligent in her duty of work. Above the front door was a frieze that depicted flowers entwined in leaves, she brushed the frieze before she cleaned the brass door knob. She took pride in scrubbing the steps that led to the door. She would stand back and look at her hard work and say, "An entrance fit for a Queen." Mary was not allowed to enter the elegant entrance to number 10, Dominick Street, she used the back entrance. Through an oak gate and up the path of the walled garden and to the back door that lead to the scullery and kitchen. In the main hallway were red and black floor tiles and a sweeping mahogany stair case. To the right was the drawing room and library. Mary loved cleaning this room. She liked to feel the books and would open the books and look in wonder at the words. She breathed in the leather and wished she could read.

One morning, Mrs Ackerman found Mary holding one of the books. "Morning, Mary." Mary jumped and, in the process, dropped the book.

"Oh, I am so sorry Mrs Ackerman, I did not see you there."

"Do not worry, Mary, I know you were doing no harm, can you read Mary?"

Mary blushed and replied, "No I cannot read, I just like holding the books, turning the pages, seeing all the words and I like the smell of the leather…" Mary stopped, she knew her place and thought she said too much.

Mrs Ackerman's heart melted. "Mary, would you like me to teach you?"

Mary nodded.

"We can come to an arrangement, let's say on Friday

at 3pm. I will teach you for half an hour."

Mary's heart sang and she gasped, "Thank you, thank you so much."

Mrs Ackerman taught Mary to read and Mary loved every moment, she could not wait for Friday afternoons. As Mary succeeded in her reading, her confidence grew and she began to grow fond of Mrs Ackerman.

One cold frosty morning, Patrick Caffery was trotting past number 10, Dominick Street, following his and his horse's breath, when some of his load which was coal fell from the cart. "Way, way, bugger!" Patrick said as he pulled on the reins.

Mary was brushing the frieze down, turned around startled. "Watch your language."

"Sorry Missus," Patrick said. He called the horse 'bugger' because the carter was frustrated, the horse was defiant, it lacked discipline and this would annoy Patrick. "Excuse me, missus, I am so sorry for me language but I have noticed you for a while. I like the look of you, would you join me in a stroll on Sunday?"

Mary pulled her white pinafore around her, to protect her from this small man with the sallow complexion and eyes of hazel green or were they hazel brown, she decided green

19

not brown. "The nerve of you, you use language like that and then ask me to go walking with you?"

"That's right. Let me know where you live and I will be there 2 pm on Sunday."

Mary, stunned and speechless, stared at the young man with the toothy smile. She smiled and replied, "The nerve of you."

"Yes, the nerve to ask you to go walking with me at 2 pm on Sunday?"

"I did not say yes." Mary felt the frost nip at her feet and her finger tips, she looked up to the sparkling blue sterile sky, then down to the carter and his cheeky grin. She noticed his smile and felt strange inside and slightly dizzy. Despite the cold her heart melted and to her surprise she said, "Yes, you can call on me at number 2 Kavanagh's Court, off Bow Street."

He frowned and coughed. "I will be there 2 pm on Sunday." He thought to himself, *"Be Jeysus she lives in Kavanagh's Court how come I never saw her before."* He cleaned up his mess and re-bagged the coal, grabbed the reins and said, "Gee up, bugger."

Mary turned around and glared at Patrick.

"Oops, sorry missis, I forgot." *"Jeysus she's got some airs and graces that girlie from Kavanagh's Court. I like her eyes and her ladylike way, her fine white gold hair, she's the one for me."*

The Georgian houses at Kavanagh's Court were similar to Mr and Mrs Ackerman's house in style but that was where the similarity ended. Fifty to sixty families shared rooms in what were once grand buildings. Ironically it was the Ackerman's and their like that owned the building. Some of the wealthy and prominent citizens of Dublin left and made their way to areas like Howth, Malahide and Sandymount, the healthy seaside towns on the outskirts of Dublin. The Ackerman's remained. The poor, poverty stricken Irish Catholics moved in, a lot came from the West of Ireland escaping the famine. The cloying desolate buildings that screamed out decay and spewed out early deaths were owned by Dublin Corporation too!

Patrick lived a few tenements up from Mary and because of the ten year gap both were unaware of each other. The couple were courting for two months when Patrick proposed to Mary. Mary refused then changed her mind when she found out the Ackerman's were leaving. Selling up because the impoverished were moving closer and the smell of Jeyes fluid was not enough to clean the stink. The Lavender man did not compensate for the smell of disease, the disease that poverty brings with the unwashed. The cook told Mary that the Ackermans were moving to Bray, to a smaller house overlooking the Irish Sea.

Mary was miles away, thinking on the marriage proposal but the thought of children terrified her. Suddenly Mrs Ackerman appeared and spoke, this made Mary jump. "Sorry dear, I did not mean to frighten you but I need to speak with you, please come into the parlour." Mrs Ackerman asked Mary to sit down and proceeded to speak. "Mary, we are moving out to Bray, to a smaller house, so we will not require your services."

Mary gulped back the tears and blew her nose in her hankie. She was devastated by this news, she had been with the family for over twenty years. "It is all right Mrs Ackerman; I am going to be married soon anyway."

Shocked and confused. Mrs Ackerman congratulated Mary. Then she said, "Mary, now you are getting married and with our new house being smaller would you like some of my old furniture?"

Mary, despite being in distress, nodded yes.

Mary and Patrick were married on August 13th, 1893 and seven days before Mary's thirty-seventh birthday. They moved to a two bedroom ground floor flat, 1, Kavanagh

Court, next door to her parents.

Mary was frugal, she had money saved, she also made Patrick aware before they were married. "I do not want to live in a one room tenement, I will have better. I witnessed my Mammy being used as a punch bag, you will never raise a fist to me!" Patrick did not argue with her. He adored his big, beautiful, buxom, bossy wife.

On her wedding day Mary was terrified because contraception did not exist, banned by the Catholic Church. She knew she had to obey her husband. Sex between man and wife could have only one purpose, procreation, not pleasure. On their wedding night, Mary lay stiff as a board. She hoped all her babies would survive, not die like her siblings. Patrick's hands plumbed deep into the crevices of his wife's shape, he smiled and happily sighed.

Their first born was a boy named James. Three days after James's birth, Mary was "Churched". Eyes of God was the role of the priest, to keep women in their place. After James's birth Mary was tarnished and impure. She had to kneel before the priest while holding a candle. Then the priest blessed and cleansed her. All Mary thought of when she looked at the priest's overly polished boots, was how her breast ached and she wanted to be home with James. Mary stifled a sob when she thought on her first born James. James was diagnosed with epilepsy and at that time children with disabilities were hidden away from society. Mary loved her son, her first born, and it broke her heart when James, aged thirteen, was pulled from her and taken to Grangegorman's hospital for the insane. Mary's remaining five children took her time but she visited James whenever she could.

Mary was brought back by a gentle knock on the door it was Esther. "Mary darling, can I come in?" Mary and Esther embraced and cried on each other's shoulders.

Five months later on a warm day in June, Esther called on Mary and told her that her husband, Alec, was admitted into Dublin Union hospital, suffering with bronchitis. Esther was relieved that Alec was in hospital because for the first time in years she could breathe and not worry if her husband found her hidden money and gambled or drank it away.

Esther, a good horse woman, was showing Maggie, Alec and little Christy the ropes of how to use a cart and to look after the horses. She turned to Mary and said "These wee children are the future carters, Mary."

"Mammy, I will pray to the blessed Mary and all the saints that Da will be well."

"How are you doing Mary?"

Mary, who was still wearing black, sighed and smiled, "Mammy I am fine, the children keep me busy."

Esther turned to her young grandchildren and instructed them in a loud voice, "Yous put the horses into the stable just like I taught you, not you Maggie, the boys only." Maggie was short, the smallest of all the children. Maggie tried her best but she was no natural around horses and Esther was aware of this.

Mary smiled and thought how Patrick would be proud of his sons, Alec and Christy and then turned to Esther and said. "Come into the kitchen, Mammy, we will have a cuppa." Both women walked into the well cleaned kitchen.

The centre point of the room was the unvarnished pine table that had been scrubbed white by Mary's hands. Maggie washed her hands and remembered not to wipe her hands in her white pinafore and then helped Essie with the cream embroidered table cloth that Maggie embroidered. Esther whispered to Mary, "Maggie may not be good with horses but she is a natural with a needle." The cloth floated from the girls' hands down onto the table. They then placed their mother's best tea cups and put a freshly baked fruit cake in the middle. The pleasant fruity aroma filled the room.

"Look at the children, Mary, what a fine healthy brood you

have, well, Essie looks a bit pale but she always looked pale. They will help you over the loss of Patrick."

"Mammy, now Patrick has gone to heaven with all the saints, God bless him, the good man he was, I am thinking of having James home, I want him out of Grangegormans. Every time I visit James it breaks my heart. I want him home where he belongs."

Esther stared at Mary, and then smiled. "God bless you Mary, I understand, you are a good woman you know. Josephine Mary has been in Richmond House[1]. It's a terrible place. But what can I do? Josephine Mary is so strong willed. Denis has another black eye where she clouted him again, that man is terrified of her, God bless him. Do you know, Mary, when I visited Josephine at Richmond House she behaved like a frightened child, desperate to get from that God forsaken place. I know it's the drink. I would give anything to have me daughter back before the tragic loss of her two children. Alec told me to leave her be, let her go to hell in her own way. He can talk, the villain he is." Both women stared into their tea cups.

"Mammy did you hear about Mrs Kean? She went to the pawn shop and only handed in a brick wrapped in news paper and Mr Solliman took it. He's a saint. Can a Jew be a

---

[1] *Richmond House was the annex of Grangegorman,s.*

saint? Well I think he is, he never judges anyone, you know."

"Mrs Kean must have been desperate her fella is always down the pub. She looks worn out and all those kiddies. She said to me thank God for the church, the only place where I can get a bit of peace and quiet. Poor woman, my heart bleeds for her. Well, Mary, I can't be sat here all day gassing, I have to go and visit himself."

Esther steered her way through the busy city of Dublin. Nearing the hospital she felt a strange sensation, a feeling of foreboding. Children playing distracted her. A boy with a gap where his teeth should have been said, "A penny to look after your horse, missus?" Esther, with a laugh in her voice, handed the reins and said, "You been getting the back of me hand, yer little villain."

Esther walked to the entrance of the hospital to a lot of commotion. Nuns and nurses were rushing about in their business. Walking down the corridor, Doctor Sullivan saw Esther before she saw him. In hushed tones he said. "Mrs Caffery, I need to talk to you."

Esther reacted nervously, "Josephine been in and playing up again? I am really sorry if it's me daughter."

The doctor led Esther into a quiet room. "Mrs Caffery, your husband tried to get out of bed and, with his chest being weak, his poor heart could not take the strain and gave out."

Esther stared blankly at the doctor, she thought Alec had bronchitis. She was not thinking right and her mind flooded with guilt and grief. "I must tell me daughters, Sarah and Josephine, Patrick me son is not here now." Her tears dripped on to the tiled floor creating small dark circles. The doctor looked on helplessly. The doctor's heart filled with sorrow for Esther, he knew she was a hard working woman who had a terrible burden with her daughter Josephine's alcoholism. The doctor was a very compassionate man who empathised with the working class of Dublin.

Once outside Esther gave the boys a penny for looking after her cart. The cheeky boy noticed a difference in Esther. "Hey, missus are you all right?" She did not hear him. She sailed through Dublin Town. A setting sun made a glowing exit, a flock of crows were giving a display but Esther was elsewhere.

She arrived at Red Cow Lane numb with shock. She nervously walked the horse and cart into the yard. The minute Mary opened the door she knew something was wrong. Esther choked, "He's gone, Mary."

Mary instructed her children, Essie and Maggie, to go and get their Auntie Sarah. And for Chrissie to go and fetch Auntie Josephine or Uncle Denis. Mary took her mother-in-law into the back room. Esther sobbed, "I am where you were five months ago, Mary." Mary suddenly became alarmed. Esther had no money for the funeral, it went on Patrick's funeral.

Sarah came running in crying and comforted her mother. Mary left them alone in their grief. She stumbled to the kitchen heavily burdened. Chrissie barged in shouting, "No Auntie Josephine, mammy, only Uncle Denis who is wearing another black eye." The children looked at their poor Uncle.

"If ever a man has suffered he has," their mother uttered under her breath. Denis, a thin nervous man, looked terrible. Josephine had pushed him over the edge, he was terrified of her.

"Sorry Mary, I have not seen Josephine for two days," Denis quietly informed his sister-in-law. "Do not worry Denis, would you like a cup of tea?"

Mary whispered to Chrissie, "Make Uncle Denis tea and stay with the children. I am going out to look for your auntie."

Mary took her shawl and slipped out of the house unnoticed. Dying embers of the setting sun gave a warm glow to Dublin. Mary felt the heat from the walls of the properties as she passed by. Mary knew there were four pubs

29

in the vicinity. She opened the door to the first pub, Carolan's, no sign of Josephine, only two men smoking their pipes and three outside playing pitch and toss. She made her way to The Ship Inn, the stale smell of beer and tobacco nearly knocked her off her feet. She heard Josephine before she saw her, "Feck off, I never liked yer pub anyway!"

Josephine staggered towards the exit and through bleary eyes she saw her sister-in-law. She stopped, rubbed her eyes and looked again. "Mary is that you?" Her dress was filthy, her hands and face needed a good wash and as Mary drew near, the stale smell of urine and beer made her retch. However, Mary had compassion for Josephine. She witnessed her fall from grace and she knew Josephine died mentally when Jane her daughter died. Jane was born the same year as Maggie.

"Josephine, you are wanted at home and I have come to fetch you."

"Oh Mary, yer so kind and all those children, you are a saint. Let's just have a wee one before we go home?" Josephine slurred.

Mary smiled and held out her hand, later both walked across the moon lit yard. Above, a blanket of stars twinkled down. Josephine saw the full moon and sang. "I see the moon…"

Mary smiled and said "Josephine, no singing tonight." Mary held Josephine's hand as they both entered the kitchen. Esther was sat with her daughter Sarah and Sarah's husband, James Boyce. Chrissie had just put the kettle back on. Home-made cake in the centre of the table left uneaten. Maggie, Alec and Christy hid in the stables, too many women and tears. Josephine staggered towards her husband Denis who was sat in the corner out of the way.

"Where did you get that shiner from?" Denis jumped up and moved away from his wife. Esther stood up and composed herself. "Josephine, I need to talk to you."

Josephine staggered towards her mother. The stench of stale booze hung in the air. Josephine slurred "Mammy, why you on your own and where's Da?"

Esther moved from the table and walked towards her daughter, she held her hand out and Josephine took it and smiled. She loved her mother, even roaring drunk she loved her. Both women went into the other room. It was dark but the lamp lighter had just lit the lamp and created an orange glow inside. Esther turned to her daughter. "Josephine, your father has gone to heaven and is now with Patrick and all the saints." Josephine laughed, laughed out loud. Then stopped and began to howl and wail. Esther grabbed Josephine. She was crying too, the burden of her husband and Josephine's

31

alcoholism had taking its toll on Esther.

Josephine's blue eyes were swimming in alcohol, she tried hard to focus on her mother. Snot ran down her face, passed her mouth and hung there. Her tear stained face was red, red from hyper tension. Josephine was fighting the demon within. She felt it rise, she needed a drink, she could not cope. Esther took her hankie from her sleeve and wiped the snot and tears away from her daughter's face.

Josephine Mary

Patrick's sister, Josephine, was married to Denis Mahoney. Denis was sixteen years older than Josephine and both were devastated by the tragic deaths. Denis continued to love Josephine but she did not love him back.

"GOD, MY HEAD! I FEEL AWFUL, I NEED A FECKING DRINK!" Josephine yelled at her husband.

"Josephine you have not been home in five days, your clothes are filthy and you have sores all over you."

"God, Denis, don't preach to me. Feck off and leave me alone."

Josephine walked out on Denis again! He cried after her but she was not listening. He looked around the room with its sparse furniture. He saw his reflection in the cracked mirror, noticed his skin was pale and his hair was receding. His huge teeth reminded him of tombstones. He walked over to the Georgian window and watched his wife stagger down the street. He was full of rheumatism, his clothes hung on him and he often thought about giving up, but deep down he had to be there for his wife. He watched her turn the corner out of Kavanagh's Court and sighed.

Josephine was making her way into town to Bewley's

café. Alcoholism had stripped her of dignity and self respect. She stood outside the prospering restaurant, took out her begging tin and cried out to people passing by. "Any money, mister, for me and me three kids? The old fella's left me."

The policemen heard Josephine before they saw her. They stopped, and with a look of exasperation, the one sighed. "Hello, Josephine, you know begging is a criminal offence."

"Ah, feck off and leave me alone."

The two police officers dragged Josephine to the police station. At the station, the Sergeant looked up to heaven when he saw her. "Josephine how many times... God, you stink." He backed away from her. "She is not staying here, get her off to Richmond House. They can sort her out. AGAIN!"

Her dress was dirty her body stank of stale biscuits and urine, her bun had come undone and her fingernails were encased in filth. Her heart raced, and her palms sweated, she needed a drink. None of the officers wanted to touch her but they had to get her out of the police station and to Richmond House. Josephine was five feet six inches tall and skin and bone. She reacted the only way she knew, through violence. She grabbed the policeman by his hair and tried to knee him in the balls but was caught from behind and frog-marched out of the station and thrown in the wagon.

Richmond House was an uninviting grey-brick building and was part of Grangegorman's hospital for the insane. On the roof stood a four-sided Roman numeral clock and in the middle of the building stood an arch with a metal gate. Josephine was dragged along the cobble stones towards a large wooden door. The door was opened by staff. Josephine was like a wild animal and it took four members of staff to get her into the large communal bathroom.

The craving for alcohol had stripped her of any sense or logic and her body ached and sweated for the drink. She began to hallucinate and saw spiders crawling from the walls. The stern staff, with their white starched pinafores stripped her of her clothing, while she shouted and wailed like a banshee and fought off the spiders that she thought were crawling all over her.

They scrubbed her clean, cut her long infested hair and rubbed a solution into her scalp to kill the head lice. Two members of staff held her down while they cut her fingernails. The staff decided to sedate her with potassium bromide. She was sedated for three days.

Josephine looked around the twenty-bed ward and thought she had gone to hell. Everywhere was grey, even the gown she was wearing was light grey. "Ah, Josephine, you are with us now?" said a poker-faced nurse.

"Please can I go home? My husband will wonder where I am and me mammy and Da." Josephine acted meek and mild. However, she was a good manipulator. Anxiety was at her throat. Without alcohol she had to feel and the last thing she wanted was to feel.

The nurse gave her sulphonal to ease her pain and the anxiety. Then the nurse sniffed and coldly said, "Josephine you need to eat some food. You have not eaten and we need you to eat to build up your strength. When you stay at Richmond you need to work for your bed and treatment. It is not free!"

Josephine thought, *I am in Richmond, oh God, Grangegorman again!* She began to cry. She had not cried in two years. Her tears flowed. "Ay, come on missy, no tears in here," said the painfully thin nurse with the unsmiling face. The nurse returned with some kind of soup that Josephine had no appetite for. She immediately stopped crying and wiped her eyes with the back of her hand and hid her grief again. She looked around her and saw a woman sat on the edge of a chair, rocking back and forth, pulling at her own hair and screaming. This terrified Josephine Mary, everything that moved frightened her. Again she pleaded with the nurse

to let her go home and she promised to never drink again.

Night time came, casting its shadow along the grey
stone floor. Josephine did not sleep because of the cries from
some of the women who were deeply distraught, one howled,
and this petrified her and kept her awake.

Morning arrived. The sun added some light and warmth to
the sad despairing, unforgiving ward. Josephine gingerly got
out of bed and made her way to the communal bathroom. Her
thin body was emaciated by alcohol. Her bare foot hit the
cold from the stone floor, this startled her. She had not been
startled since her daughter Jane died in her arms. She used
the communal toilet and then washed her hands and face. She
saw her reflection in the mirror, her skin was yellow, she
rolled her tongue round her toothless mouth, saw her nose
was twisted and broken. She staggered back to the cold,
sterile ward and the insane animal sounds that came from the
women.

The image of Jane and her doll-like face haunted
Josephine. She scratched at her arms but her nails were cut
and she could not pierce the skin to release the buried guilt.
Josephine left Jane for a minute to go and borrow some sugar
from her next door neighbour, Mrs Kelly, when she heard a

scream that could be heard in Kingstown. Josephine shouted, "Oh my God, the fire guard, the bloody fire guard!" She ran into the room that she shared with her husband Denis and their little girl. Their only child was lying on the bare wooden floorboards, badly burnt. The kettle that had been full of water was to the side, its contents on Jane, who was dying from shock. Mrs Kelly grabbed a cloth, plunged it into the cold bucket and covered the poor child. It was too late. Jane died just past her first birthday in early March 1900.

Josephine disappeared into the deepest part of her mind, beyond pain and grief, to where no one could reach her. Denis and her parents tried to help her whenever possible, but she had gone too far to be saved by anyone. They say the little mite's heart gave out due to the shock. She despised herself for not being there for her daughter.

Her arms still ached for her and the prayer book that was given as a gift at Jane's christening was still in Josephine's possession. She looked down the length of the ward to the large windows. Anxiety soared through her, her heart raced and sweat poured from her. The urge to run and jump through one of the windowpanes beckoned. She slumped back down when she saw Denis coming towards her. Her battered frail husband whose love was not enough for Josephine. "Oh Denis, please take me home."

"Josephine, I cannot, they have put you here for your own safety, you are a danger to yourself and others."

"Denis, I will be good." She pleaded with her husband.

Within three days, Josephine was discharged wearing a dress that was too big for her thin, frail body. Her fine, mousy brown hair shone and her eyes that were blurred and red were now blue grey. She left Richmond Asylum with her mother and her husband. It was her mother who often bailed her daughter out. Paid the cost of a non pauper and often paid her fines too.

Jane was not Josephine's first born. Her first born was another girl who was stillborn. Josephine knew there was something wrong because the little one that was inside her had stopped moving. She had to go along with the pregnancy knowing that her baby was dead. This broke her heart. A year later Jane was born and the loss of Jane destroyed Josephine. She committed the carnal sin of not letting her husband sleep with her. She also turned her back on the Catholic Church. After, people blamed her saying it was her fault the child had died. Josephine died mentally and spiritually, because she could not cope with the guilt.

Death among babies and children was commonplace

in Dublin, especially in the tenements. However, some women found the grief and loss unbearable, and found no comfort or solace in the church, so they drowned their pain in alcohol. Josephine Mary Mahony died at the age of thirty eight, of no fixed abode. In her short tragic life, she was homeless three times, and admitted seven times into Richmond Asylum. She also committed seventeen criminal offences.

Later that week, Alexander Caffery came home to Bow Street and to the rooms that they had shared for many years. Alec was laid out in the living room, wearing a white shroud with black rosary beads entwined in his hands. Esther and her son-in-law, James Boyce, sat beside the open coffin and were in deep conversation. "James what could I do, Mary did not have enough money to bury Patrick…." She stopped made a sign of the cross, wiped a stray tear.

James shifted in his chair coughed and said, "Sarah and I have some money saved, we will pay the cost."

Esther cried, "Thank you James, thank you, I will do my best to pay you back."

"Well, Mammy, there is a way you can pay me back but we will talk about this after the funeral."

Esther sat alone with her thoughts and remembered

the first time Alec kissed her. She and Alec were running through meadows bare foot, her dark hair was flowing in the breeze. She ran from him giggling. Alec caught up with her, she fell, he knelt down and kissed her, she had never been kissed before. She would give anything to bring those happy carefree days back before the drink took hold.

Esther had to carry on in her role as the main breadwinner. She thought of the time when they got married. Someone had given her a handkerchief as a wedding present that could be turned into a baby's bonnet, a bonnet for her first born. Patrick was her first born, she remembered singing to Patrick a little ditty she knew. "How many miles to Dub-li-n three score and ten. Will we be there by candle light? Yes and back again. Hupp, hupp, my little horse, hupp hupp again!"

Esther sighed and then realised Josephine was not among the family. She was too overcome with grief to be concerned about her wayward daughter. A sob escaped from her mouth but no one noticed they were too busy singing 'Danny Boy.'

Esther gave part of her round to her son-in-law, James Boyce, as payment for her husband's funeral. The other part of her round she gave to her grandsons, Alec and Christy.

Alec and Christy had a contract with Dublin Corporation and this was only given to trustworthy people. In the days before trucks and lorries when the standard mode of transport of goods was horse and cart. The two brothers kept their round and the yard going till the early nineteen sixties. January 1913, Esther Caffery died aged sixty-one, from bronchitis and was buried in an unmarked grave.

Mary visited the priest to discuss James being home with his family. The priest nodded and told Mary there was a process that she had to go through. That week Mary visited James, he was not at the visitors' room, no one was there. She left the room and walked towards the double doors that led to the communal ward. As she opened the door, the stink of faeces and urine nearly knocked her off her feet. Some people wore strait jackets, one man was punching the wall and in the middle laying in a foetal position on his bed, was her dark haired handsome son, James. Mary was shocked, then anger kicked in. She ran to James's bed, hugged her handsome dark haired son. James shaking and tears streaming down his terrified face asked, "Mammy when am I going home?"

A tall thin nurse was making her way towards Mary and demanded what she was doing on the ward. Mary shouted, "How dare you question me when my son is living in fear."

With that the matron arrived. "Mrs Caffery, I can explain."

Mary raised her hand and said, "You get away from me and my son now!" Mary held James's hand and both left the hell on earth ward. Mary took James home to be cared for by his own loving family.

Maggie turned the corner of her street, pulled the ribbon from her waist length hair, letting her hair flow. She was holding her friend Lily's hand. Both turned left away from the school gates. They were making their way to Phoenix Park that was four miles away for a lesson in freedom and climbing trees. The Park had a huge lake, wooded area and a zoo, a haven full of wonder. Maggie had no fear, she just wanted to play. She would run like the wind among the trees with her friend Lily. Lily struggled to keep up with her boisterous friend. "Come on, Lily, I will race you, race you to the top of the hill"

Maggie wore boots, Lily's feet were bare but Maggie often took her boots off to be like Lily. Both girls lay on their sides, linked hands, played roly-poly and rolled down the green slopes. They laughed and giggled to their hearts' content. Despite Lily's poverty she loved school, she took everything in like a sponge. Not today. She wanted to let the child in her out to play. Lily liked Maggie, she liked her enthusiasm and her humour, most of all she liked the way Maggie accepted her.

Barefooted, grass tickling their toes, they both laid down. Maggie saw the outline trace of the moon in day time. She pointed up to the sky, both girls stood up and danced and sang. The girls' laughter floated on the wind and onto the ears of Father Flynn. Father Flynn was portly shaped with a bluish complexion. He boomed at the two young girls, "Good afternoon, you two, and why are you not in school?" The girls blushed with embarrassment at being caught by a priest.

"Sorry, father, we just wanted a stroll on this fine afternoon," said Maggie, acting as if she was a grown up.

The priest replied in a stern voice, "Now, I will turn a blind eye this time but if I catch yous two again your parents will be told. That will bring shame on your family and do you want that to happen?"

"Sorry, father," said the girls in unison.

1913 lockout

There was unrest in Dublin and the unions were not happy.
Dublin's working class boil was ready for lancing and James
Connolly, leader of 'The Citizen Army', along with the
charismatic leader of 'The Irish General Workers Union',
James Larkin, was waiting in the wings with a hot poultice.
Chrissie and Maggie both took part in the '1913 Lockout'.
Both greatly admired Larkin and both were aggrieved about
the sacking of tram workers because they wanted to join a
union. Chrissie worked at 'Jacobs' biscuit factory. Maggie
worked at Leinster Sewing Factory. Both came out in support
of the sacked tram workers. The Catholic charity, 'The
Vincent De Paul Society,' was against the strikers. They
referred to them as atheists and so did their mother Mary.
However, the British TUC had given £93,000 to help the
strikers and their families.

Christina was born in 1895, Patrick and Mary's first
daughter. Chrissie, as she was known to her family, was a
pretty child and grew into a beautiful woman. When her
father died in 1910, Chrissie was the main breadwinner in the
family. She was feisty, she wanted change, a socialist in the
making. She admired women like Delia Larkin, Agnes

O'Farrelly, Hannah Sheehy Skeffington. She heard these women speak at 'The Liberty Hall' and she remembered the last speech. *"Nothing was granted, not your vote, not your education, not your daily wage"*.

She thought back to the ladies' dining room at Jacobs's factory, where she worked as a packer. Wrapped in her white pinafore watching a young, petite girl of sixteen, Rosie Hackett. Rosie was a messenger at Jacobs and was a girl ahead of her time. The injustice and poverty of Dublin's working class drove Rosie on. Rosie put word out about women joining a union. The Irish Transport & General Workers Union (ITGWU) Chrissie's ears pricked up at this. First she had to get past her biggest obstacle, her mother!

Mother and daughter stood in the kitchen. The cold from the flagstones eased the heat, the opened door brought a pleasant breeze and the dust from the yard. This made Chrissie sneeze, she wiped her nose, clipped a strand of hair back, while her mother gave her an angry look. The words of William Martin Murphy, business man and JP, rang in Chrissie's ears, *"I question the wisdom of allowing unskilled and semi-skilled workers to join a union because they generally lacked intelligence."* His words incensed Chrissie. "Mammy, I had to come out, it is unfair. We should have the choice and the right to join a union. A union can help and protect us in our fight for a better wage and working conditions."

"Christina, I rely on you, Essie and Maggie's wage for the rent. James's health is not good and he picks up everything that passes through Dublin and to top it all, that English woman Dora Montefiore, wants to take the poor children of Dublin over to England and have them live with Protestant families. Father O'Reilly told us all about it in mass."

"Mammy, you do not understand, she is on our side. Children are starving and she is helping us, unlike this government and the rich business men who own the tenements." Chrissie was frustrated, she wanted more than anything for her mother to understand. She knew her mother was devout and the church came before anything. However, she was not aware how the strike terrified her mother. Her mother thought if there was no money, the rent would not be paid and they would have to go back to living in the tenements and sharing a toilet with 50 other tenants.

Mary coughed as she recalled her memories of Kavanagh's Court. The stench of poverty, the one room and the red velvet curtain that split the room in two. On the other side of the curtain, and sleeping on a shared mattress, were her six children. Mary had the income of Essie and Maggie's wage and a small amount from the boys' delivery round.

She had a mangle that she could hire out but that was futile because people did not have the money. Mary stroked the wood on the chaise lounge and sighed. "What am I to do?"

"Mammy, please, we have no choice, they locked us out and the only way back in is to sign a pledge that we will not belong to a union. The union is our way out of poverty!" Both women looked at each other, their faces were strained from the arguing. Chrissie left, slamming the kitchen door shut, making James jump. She made her way to 'Liberty Hall' to help feed the poor. When not demonstrating, Chrissie often helped out at the soup kitchens at Liberty Hall. She felt at home there, she liked being around like minded people.

Unknown to her family, Chrissie had a beau. His name was Michael Morrissey, he was a radical like Chrissie and a member of 'The Citizen Army.' 'The Citizen Army' protected striking workers against the police. They made a handsome couple, she was an open faced beauty, he with thick jet black hair and square jawed with republican leanings, a follower of James Connolly. Chrissie fell for him instantly.

At home sat Mary with her pride and fear of being poor. She had to decide which piece of furniture she was going to pawn.

Later that week Chrissie met with her friend Lizzy, Lizzy, a
thin wiry girl, a true radical and, like Rosie Hackett, a woman
ahead of her time. She inspired Chrissie. Both women now
wore the red hand badge of the union ITGWU with pride on
their blouses. "I am a bit nervous Lizzy; I hope there is no
trouble now that we know that men from England are over
here taking our jobs."

"Chrissie, it is not just the English, it is our own scab
workers from the far West of Ireland!"

They arrived at Bishop Street to chaos, both stood
bewildered among the confusion when they were turned
away by the police. Both rebels were incensed and through
frustration Chrissie shouted. "God! Lizzy, what do we do
now?"

"On Sunday there is going to be a mass rally, a show
of unity, a united front. Chrissie, we are going to be there and
be a part of Irish history!"

At home Chrissie opened the door, Essie was standing in the
kitchen. She noticed that her sister had been crying. "What's
wrong, Essie, is James all right?"

"He's grand, but it's Mammy," Essie meekly replied.

49

Chrissie's heart missed a beat.

"Is Mammy all right?" the eldest girl asked.

"Mammy is beside herself, I have never seen her like this before," Essie said through tears.

Chrissie found her mother in the back room, gazing out the window, a damp hankie in her hand.

"Mammy, Mammy what is wrong?" she said with concern.

"What is wrong, what is wrong? Look around you girl," Mary said choked with anger and shame. Chrissie looked in disbelief, her mother's precious chaise lounge and other pieces of furniture were gone. "Alec and Christy helped me put the furniture on to the cart and take it to Mr Spellman, the pawn broker. The shame of it all! I had to join a queue that was nearly a mile long."

Over the next four days the house was unbearable. Then Maggie's sewing factory came out in support! Dublin was at a standstill, nothing moved only the scabs that scurried about under the protection of the police.

Sunday morning, 26th August, 8am. The Caffery family were walking to church. Mary held James's hand, the two boys ran ahead and the three sisters walked behind. Maggie turned to Chrissie and said, "Jeysus, it is stifling heat, what will it be like later?"

Chrissie smiled at her little sister and replied, "Maggie, we will be too excited to think of the heat."

Inside the ice cold church, the priest preached and dished out his opinions on starving children being sent to Protestant homes in England, while the congregation nodded in awe-filled agreement except the three Caffery sisters.

The family left the cold stone, stale, candle waxed, incense smelling church to be greeted by a scorching sun. Mary, her boys and Essie went one way. Chrissie and Maggie to the protest. Mary let out a deep sigh, shook her head. She could not understand her daughter's behaviour.

The two sisters met up with Lizzy. Lizzy in her excitement did not notice Maggie. "Hi, Chrissie, how are you doing? Oh hi, Maggie, welcome to your first demo. Are you excited?" Maggie nodded.

Chrissie cried, "Be Jeysus, we are going to be part of Irish history!"

O' Connell Street, the heart of Dublin, was heaving with people out for the cause. A proletarian cause for workers who wanted justice and a right to join a Union, altogether with their banners held high with Larkin's words, **'An Injury to one is a Concern for All,'** blazed across. Chrissie looked up to the cloudless sky, noticed the sun shone in union. They seemed to be moving without knowing. Then suddenly the crowd became more vocal, shouting that led to screaming, followed by offensive language and aggressive pushing. Chrissie shouted, "Lizzie some of the men are carrying bats hidden under their clothing"

"They have no other choice, Chrissie," yelled Lizzie above the racket.

For the first time Chrissie felt afraid, afraid for her own safety and Maggie's. The two sisters' bellies churned when they heard the crunching sound of wood meeting bone and gun shots being fired. Lizzie saw the look of fear in her friend's eyes. Chrissie cried in terror, "I want to get out from here. I cannot breathe. I am being crushed!" Maggie, aged fourteen, looked around her with wide eyed excitement. Suddenly Lizzie disappeared into the crowd and both sisters were lost among the protesters that were being fenced in by the Dublin Metropolitan Police, contained for their own safety. Chrissie's mouth was dry, then in horror she saw the police attack her comrades when they should have been protecting them. Chrissie felt suffocated by the smell of fear and the heat from other people's bodies. Then she realised Maggie was no longer with her. She let out a scream, "Maggie!" Then a hand appeared and grabbed her by her shoulder, "Get off me, get off me!" she cried.

"It's alright, it's me, Michael." Michael Morrissey was looking out for Chrissie, he was aware the situation was becoming more dangerous and he feared for Chrissie. He threw his bat away and stayed by her side.

Chrissie shouted, "God, Michael, I thought you were rozzers."

"Keep hold of my hand and do not let go. Do as I say and you will be safe."

"No, I can't, I have lost Maggie, my little sister, I need to find her."

Michael grabbed Chrissie's arm and marched Chrissie away from the danger, away from the violent angry crowd. A mile from the scene they stopped. Chrissie held onto Michael and sobbed on the rebel's shoulder. Maggie was four years younger than Chrissie but was more outspoken and rebellious than her elder sister. Through tearful eyes Chrissie saw her short, petite sister running towards them. A policeman was running after her and shouted at her to stop, but Maggie kept running. She caught up with the lovers and the three ran like the wind through the back streets of Dublin and home.

Outside the gate they looked at each other and laughed, Michael gasped, "What an escape. God! You Caffery sisters can run."

Chrissie knocked on the door. Essie opened the door, she heard giggling then saw her two sisters red faced, glinting with perspiration. Essie noticed the young man by her sister's side. "Essie, this is Michael Morrissey, Michael, this is Essie, my sister."

"How do you do, miss," Michael said politely.

Essie nodded and stood aside to let them in but whispered, "Chrissie how did it go, was it good? Were there many there? Be careful, Mammy is not happy."

They continued through to the kitchen. Mary was by the stove, elated by her outing to Vincent de Paul. She preached, "I have given a donation to Vincent de Paul to stop the children from going to Protestant homes in England."

"Mammy this is Michael."

"How are you, Mrs Caffery?"

"Oh! Another atheist friend of yers, I see," Mary spat the words at Michael.

Michael clenched his fists and spoke, "Mrs Caffery, do you know where we have been this very day, fighting for our jobs, demonstrating for a better pay and a right to join a union while your friends collect for the starving children and protect them from the Protestant English religion yet turn a blind eye to British scab workers coming here, taking our jobs and the very food from the mouths of starving kids.

Please do not preach to me for being an atheist but shame on you for concealment. Now that is what I call a sin!"

The house was deathly silent. The three girls stared open mouthed at Michael Morrissey They were shocked that he dared to address their mother in such a way. The last thing on Michael's mind was showing respect to his elders, he was an angry frustrated young man. There were many like him too. Michael continued with his tirade, "Why can't people see that if proletarians fight back and stand together, we can really conquer the poverty and replace the system with a fair wage. The fecking hardest battle we have is with our own people and the bleeding church."

Mary was shocked and speechless. Before she could reply, Michael turned and walked away. Just as he got to the door he turned to Chrissie, kissed her on the cheek, saying, "Meet me on Tuesday the same place."

The door slammed, the four women jumped. Mary looked at her daughter and through gritted teeth she said, "Christina, you are lucky that I don't hit you with the back of me hand for looking so love struck, and falling for an atheist. That man is not allowed in my house as long as I am alive!" Chrissie did not hear what her mammy said. She was in love with the rebel.

She met Michael at a rally, six months previous, he

was there as a member of 'The Citizen Army.' He saw her pale green eyes, he had never seen eyes that colour before. They mesmerised him. They stared at each other in awe. "Do not move, I will see you later." As he left he brushed his hand along her right cheek. No man had ever looked at her that way before and no one had ever inspired her like Michael Morrissey. Michael did not care who he offended, he was fighting for the cause. This put Michael in good stead for a better cause, the cause for a free Ireland, a Republican Ireland!

Crisp, cold autumn morning, Essie was in work, Christy and Alec in school, James inside with his Mother. Chrissie and Maggie were in the yard wringing bedding out for their mother. Mary, in her wisdom, thought if her daughters refuse to go to work they can work here for her! Chrissie, sleeves rolled up, sweat at her brow turned the mangle handle. Maggie pulled the sheets and woollen blanket. Chrissie stopped and softly spoke out of earshot of their mother. "Maggie, I know things will get worse, but we will get through this."

Maggie, chilblained hands on her hips said, "I will never sign that document and sell my soul, Chrissie. James Connolly's words are still here." Maggie stopped and pointed to her head. "Here, in my mind. He regards us women as comrades in arms with the men. I want better than Mammy and I know you do too. Remember Connolly's words, **'That the great only appeared great because us poor were on our knees,'** Chrissie, we are not on our knees."

Chrissie sighed, "Maggie, little Maggie, my young sister such a wise girl."

Later that same week Mary and James left the house for the four minute walk to Church Street, and to 'Father Mathew Hall,' for a social gathering of music. Both breathed in the early late sunny autumn September air. At the hall there were many voices chatting and laughter filled the room. Suddenly all went quiet, outside was a slow rumbling sound like thunder and then a cannon roar. Someone at the back of the hall opened the door to see if it was raining. A gasp and a shout, "Oh my God, number 66 is collapsing."

A panicked crowd rushed out of the hall. One was a young lad called Hugh Salmon. He worked at Jacobs. He rushed out to what was left of the room he shared with his family. The young lad was insanely heroic in rescuing members of his family, tragically, on his last return trip to fetch his little sister Elizabeth, the building collapsed and both perished.

Maggie and her two sisters heard the noise and ran out to the yard to be greeted with a thick air of smoke and debris. Outside they bumped into their Mammy and James, both were emotional. Their Mammy blurted out, "It's terrible." The three sisters arrived at Church Street to cries of the young and old, relatives crying and shouting, and two collapsed houses spewed across the street.

The fire brigade along with fifty Dublin Corporation workers arrived to the carnage and chaos. People were told to be quiet so that they could listen for any signs of life. After a short time the men, armed with pick axes, shovels and crow bars began to dig among debris. People looked on helplessly. Essie began to comfort those who were deeply distressed.

Night time drew near and the lack of lighting hampered the rescue. Maggie and Chrissie ran home to collect candles. As they arrived back they noticed the church hall was lit up, others had brought lanterns and some lit candles. The rescue operation went on for hours. As dawn broke, the following day revealed the terrible aftermath of the collapsed tenement building. Seven died and a hundred were homeless. Number 66, Church Street collapsed, warning residents at number 67.

These diseased riddled, decaying, strictly unsound buildings, were owned by Dublin Corporation and three members of the Corporation owned sixty-four buildings between them. Shockingly, nearly all were unfit for human habitation.

The Caffery family, like most of Dublin, struggled though the six month 'Lockout' and a very stormy bleak winter! The strikers were forced back to work because many families were literally starving. Murphy's paper, the 'Irish Independent' deemed striking, broken men evil because they did not support their suffering wives and hungry children.

Dublin, 18th January, 1914, the working class returned to work, spirits cracked but not broken! Within a short time the ITGWU became the largest Union in Dublin. Within a few years it had become a national movement of over 120,000 members and the first moves were made to tackle the TENEMENT problem!

1914, First World War

Mary had taken James to visit relatives, Essie was in work, the boys out in the yard were stacking the hay. Michael, Chrissie and Maggie sat in the kitchen, a draught from the back kitchen window gave a slight relief from the heated discussion and the sweet scent of fresh hay added lightness. "Is it true that Carsonite Volunteers with the help of British sympathisers in high places ran a cargo of arms ashore at Larne?" Maggie asked Michael.

Michael nodded yes, "We think they distributed them throughout Ulster by motors flying through the night."

Chrissie tartly replied, "Yes and the British Government prohibited the importation of arms into Ireland lest we should secure weapons too."

They say the first shots fired in the First World War were in Ireland, 26th July, on a beautiful warm summer's day. However, a week before on Sunday, July 19th, Dublin Volunteers were mobilised for a route march to Howth. The Volunteers were as usual being watched by the police. Only two officers knew what the day's programme was. The commander's rank and file obediently marched towards Dublin Bay. When they arrived at Baldoyal they were ordered to stop. An hour later, after refreshments, they marched back.

The following Sunday the Volunteers were again mobilised. Nearly a thousand paraded from all parts of Dublin, among them was Michael Morrissey. Some noticed the Sunday paper placard, 'International crisis between Austria and Serbia.' They began to whisper, "If there is a World War, it is not our war." Volunteers did not march to Baldoyal but to the great hill of Howth. Marching towards the narrow line that links Howth to the main land. They made their way to Howth Harbour, where a small yacht was sailing.

None of the Volunteers, save perhaps three men, knew what the yacht was carrying in her hold. When the Volunteers reached the harbour they were halted. The yacht nearing the mouth of the harbour suddenly dropped her white sails and the little craft ran under the light house around the pier. The order was to double down the pier. Some of the men felt something was afoot and hurried, others followed. A small group of Rebels appeared from nowhere and guarded the foot of the pier with automatic pistols. Coast guards venturing to interfere found themselves looking into the muzzles of lethal weapons and thought better to not venture any further.

Police tried to inform Dublin but found the wire was cut. The column halted at the pier and where the little yacht was moored. Heavy batons of wood and leather wrist straps were dealt out and a hundred or so Volunteers were armed. In the summer light, straw bound objects were being handed up from the boat to those Volunteers who held the pier-head. Soon the straw was torn away and the Irish Volunteers saw their first rifles. Shrieks of joy went up! The men broke and dashed forward, eager to get arms. In a few minutes every Volunteer held a rifle in their hands.

The Volunteers marched with rifles on their shoulders through Howth, making their way back to the city, and along the way they were cheered by members of the public, holiday makers, people on tram tops. All cheered loudly! The police marched behind. At Clontarf, Volunteer cycle scouts rode back to the column with word that British soldiers had blocked the entrance to the city.

Outside Dublin, Volunteers drew up to a few feet in front of the khaki line. Disagreements ensued with the police and British army and this was taking a long time. While the arguments over technicalities carried on, the Volunteers dispersed over fields and hid their weapons. The Scottish Borders marched back to their barracks and were jeered by people who resented an attempt to disarm Nationalists, yet

Carsonites were encouraged to arms! The soldiers fired two rounds of volleys into the crowd and tragically four people were shot dead and fifty were wounded.

Michael and Chrissie were out on a late afternoon stroll walking through the park. She glanced at Michael's side profile, watched the wind play with his thick hair. It was not often Chrissie could link her arm in Michael's and walk out in the fresh air. She squeezed his arm and whispered, "I treasure these moments." Michael kissed the top of her head. "Michael, it is shocking what happened last Sunday. I was so concerned about you."

"No need to be concerned, be more concerned with Asquith who tried to gloss over the terrible tragic, incident and the murdering of innocent people."

"The rest of Ireland was appalled and infuriated, Michael."

"I know Chrissie and this is good but now this war is here. The papers are saying the war would not be a long war."

"This war is not ours."

"Tell that to John Redmond. He is seizing the opportunity by offering the use of the national controlled Irish Volunteers to help defend the shores of Ireland against enemy action, along with the Ulster Unionists, in return for their patriotic stance."

"Is it true both sides hoped to secure some positive response from the British government in support of their Irish claims?"

"Chrissie, I know in my gut Asquith will place 'The 1914 Irish Home Rule Act' on the statute book and that is where it will remain!"

Maggie opened the kitchen door and barged in to the smell of Jeyes fluid that tickled her nostrils. She rubbed her nose with the back of her hand. Her mother and her two sisters were sat in the kitchen, her two brothers Alec and Christy were out on a delivery. James sat in the corner staring at his red cheeked mother and his sisters who fascinated him.

"Oh, I just saw Mr Kenny, walking up Bow Street. You should have seen him in his British uniform, showing off and preening just like a peacock. That is until a couple of kiddies were running behind him shouting bang, bang Mister! He jumped out of his skin." Maggie bent over, and let out a belly laugh.

Mary looked at her daughter with disdain. "Maggie, where is your respect, Mr Kenny has joined the army to fight a war and I admire that man. Mrs Kenny and all her children will now have some money coming in."

Chrissie looked up from her sewing and sighed. "Mammy, it is a manipulation of the Brits using our men, knowing they are desperate for money, to fight their war! Those who hide behind desks, upper class twits! Using our working class as cannon fodder. Enticing our men with the carrot stick of a wage to join up to fight Britain's war. Our own could die!"

"Chrissie, that atheist of yours is a bad influence on you."

Maggie spoke quickly to defuse the situation. "Chrissie, would you like me to take your work skirt in for you?"

"Ah, Maggie, thank you but I am fine, I like to keep me hands busy." Chrissie was fuming with her mother's ignorant attitude but the pain in her heart distracted her. She had not seen Michael for a while.

"Chrissie, stop behaving like a love sick loon and find someone better to moon over."

"I need some air," cried Chrissie. She fled the room and went outside to the yard. The dusty cobbled yard stank of horse manure and dry straw. Her heart ached and her belly churned and she whispered, "God, if this is love, why am I not happy." The image of Michael came to her in her mind's eye and desire for him flooded her very being. He was brave and driven in the cause for a free Ireland, she wanted this too. She was proud of him despite what her mother said. "Owe!! That hurt," she said out loud to herself. She had brought her sewing out with her, and in her day dreaming she had dug the needle into her thumb. Blood trickled on to her hand, and as she looked up, Michael was looking over the yard wall.

"Hey, Missus, would you like to take a walk with me to the Park?"

Chrissie's heart jumped as she ran to him. He saw the blood and licked it from her pale white hand. They stared at each other, she noticed he had lost weight. A lock of her chestnut brown hair escaped from her bun, he stroked it and put it to his nostrils. He loved everything about her even the scent of her hair. "Well I think I can spare a few hours for me fella," she said with a laugh in her voice. It was a laugh of joy. Chrissie ran inside to the kitchen. "Hey Maggie, catch." She threw her skirt to her younger sister. "I think you will make a better job than me."

Maggie looked up and saw happiness radiate from her sister. Mary sniffed, "The atheist's turned up."

Michael saw Alec and Christy coming up towards him. "How yer doing, boys?" he said with a smile. The two brothers looked up to Michael. He was a hero to them.

66

"Grand, Michael, just grand," said Alec.

August 1st, 1915 and O' Donovan Rossa's funeral

August 1st, 1915, it was a beautiful summer's day, everyone in Dublin came to bear witness to this sad occasion. It was the funeral of one of Ireland's favourite Fenians. The great O'Donovan Rossa. Poet and school teacher, Padraic Pearse, spoke to the massive crowd:

*"They think that they have pacified Ireland. They think that they have purchased half of us and intimidated the other half. They think that they have foreseen everything, think that they have provided against everything; but the fools, the fools! - They have left us our Fenian dead, and while Ireland holds these graves, Ireland **unfree shall never be at peace.**"*

A tremendous and sustained cheer erupted from the crowd of thirty thousand people, as Padraic Pearse concluded his oration at the graveside of O'Donovan Rossa.

Maggie watched her fourteen-year-old brother, Alec, cheering wildly, with both fists pumping high in the air, and tears streaming down his face, his eyes fixated on Pearse. Eleven year old Christy had his eyes fixed on his adored older brother and as always was copying Alec. Chrissie and Essie were clapping frantically and cheering loudly.

Maggie's thoughts, as she stood amid this huge throng, were with the dead — with her father, Patrick, and grandfather, Alexander, who both died within six months of each other five years previously, and with her grandmother, Esther, who died two and half years previously.

Other ghosts flitted through her mind as Pearse saluted the huge cheering throng, — Wolf Tone, Emmet, Fitzgerald and the other Irish martyrs. Snatches of songs and lines from recitations ran through her mind:

'*Who fears to speak of 98*
Who blushes at the name'
"*At Boulavogue as the sun was setting,*
O'er the bright May meadow of Shelmalier
A rebel hand set the heather blazing
And brought the neighbours from far and near"
"*When my country takes her place among the nations of the earth, then and not till then let my epitaph be written.*"

Thomas McDonough and Tom Clark were now standing on the small platform on either side of Pearse, their hands clasped together and their arms high in the air as they turned to acknowledge the crowd all around. Maggie recalled some of the social gatherings of the tightly knit extended family. Everyone had their party-piece. Of course 'Molly Malone' and 'I'll take you home again Kathleen' were great favourites, but the stories and laments for the glorious failures of Ireland's troubled past were the best. Having listened to these stories and songs so many times, the images they conjured up ran rapidly through her mind's eye, the Normans, Cromwell, 98, the Penal Laws, Emmet's rebellion, the famine, the Fenian rebellion, and Parnell.

'And I met with Napper Tandy and he took me by the hand,
he said how's poor old Ireland and how does she stand?
She's the most distressful nation that ever has been seen,
They're hanging men and women for the wearing of the
green.'
"My aged father did me deny, And the name he gave me was
the Croppy Boy."

Maggie knew that Ireland was on the verge of something cataclysmic. The war in France had raged for almost a year now and the initial hopes that it would be all over by Christmas had long since faded. Today, France was a long way off. For as long as she could remember, Maggie had yearned for Irish freedom, the bedtime songs and stories from her parents and grandparents amounted to one thing.

"And then I prayed I yet might see, our fetters rent in twain, and Ireland long a province, be a nation once again."

From what she had heard of Pearse and what she had seen and heard today, she knew that here was a charismatic leader in the same mould as Emmet and Tone. She knew that there would be bloodshed and suffering, yet she wondered if it would all end up another glorious failure like that of Emmet, Tone and the Fenians. But most of all, she worried about the effect it would have on her family. She knew that Alec was already a convert to the cause and where Alec went, Christy was sure to follow. She said a silent prayer that it would all be over before either was old enough to participate fully.

Maggie noticed a dark haired young man standing by her eldest sister's side. Maggie knew that it was Michael, she recognised that distinctive strong jaw anywhere. Michael was part of the guard of honour around O'Donovan Rossa's remains as he lay in state in City Hall. "Afternoon, ladies," he greeted the women with a tilt of his cap. Alec and Christy were in awe of this young soldier cum rebel.

The Caffery children, Dublin and the West of Ireland were inspired and driven in the cause for a free Ireland. Listening to Pearse's speech, had a profound affect and was the catalyst for future events that would take place later in

Ireland.

It was a beautiful late summer's day with a cloudless sky as Michael and Chrissie walked arm in arm through the Park. They both stopped and listened to a blackbird singing high above on top of an oak tree. They looked at each other and smiled. Michael spoke in a serious tone, "Christina, this war is no longer our concern and Redmond siding with the Liberals seems to have got us nowhere. Home rule is now a distant memory. You know the Brotherhood opposed the war and we have done our best to prevent recruitment. Now Redmond wants to send some of our soldiers overseas. There is now a division in the Irish Volunteers. I am with Jim on this and do you know what Redmond's followers are called? 'National Volunteers'. You know I will be disappearing from time to time and I will make every effort to stay in touch whenever I can. Remember, Christina, my love is for my Country but most of all it is for you and our future children and grandchildren. I am doing this for us to have a free Ireland."

Michael had his conscription papers and he ignored them, and continued to ignore any papers from the British Government and Army. Michael was eventually summoned to court and spent 3 months in prison for refusing to fight for

Britain. It was no hardship for Michael and others. He gladly enjoyed his many weeks in prison. However Chrissie suffered. Her mother's spiteful tongue was worse than ever. Her mother referred to Michael as a coward! This remark wounded Chrissie beyond words.

A week before Easter, the Irish Tricolour was flying over the Liberty Hall as if Republicanism was already in being. The air in and around Dublin was tensed with many raids, capture of arms, strange threats and rumours filled the public's mind with the impression that something big was going to happen. Some thought the Volunteers might disarm and what resistance was there left? Dublin frizzled with fear and sensationalism!

It was a bright spring morning, new green leaf buds were unfurling on the trees. Mary Caffery and her family made their way to Easter Sunday mass. As they opened the church doors the spring flowers gave a powerful scent, overpowering the candles and incense. The coldness seeped into their bones, making Mary shiver. The family sat in pews that creaked like an old ship. Chrissie was agitated, she fidgeted with her white gloves. Maggie nudged Essie and both sisters glanced at their older sister.

Maggie whispered in Chrissie's ear, "We have a

notion that something is not right with you, and we have not seen Michael round here for a while."

Chrissie's bottom lip quivered, Essie linked her arm into her big sister's and gently guided her to the back of the church, followed by Maggie. Chrissie's eyes were cast down, tears lined her rosy cheeks, she whispered, "I am fine, just behaving like a love sick loon." She took a white linen handkerchief from her coat pocket andwiped her eyes and nose.

Michael had told Chrissie that something big might be happening, and he would not be able to see her for a while. Chrissie, a beautiful looking girl, was feisty and wanted to be part of any rebellion. She was different, a different woman from her mother's generation. She wanted to be part of the changing tide that was taking place. She knew Ireland was a ticking bomb that was waiting to go off. Chrissie wanted to be one of the many hands that pulled the pin that would release freedom and independence for Ireland! There were powerful inspirational women that inspired Chrissie and her two sisters. Women like Hannah Sheehy Skeffington, Rosie Hackett, Agnes Winifred O'Farrelly and Kathleen Lynn.

Chrissie was involved with Cumann Na mBan (League of Women who became the auxiliary to the Irish

Volunteers). Maggie and Essie both attended meetings held by Cumann na mBan. Kathleen Lynn was the first female medical student to graduate from University College Dublin. She was chief medical officer during the Easter Uprising and she inspired gentle, sensitive nursing assistant Essie.

After church the sisters heard the newspaper boy shout the headlines, "No parade today!" Chrissie stopped, took the paper from the young lad while Essie paid him. The three sisters crouched over the Irish Independent Sunday paper. Eoin MacNeill, Chairman of the Volunteers, Professor of Medieval History, a knight in shining armour and whose lover was Ireland had written in the press:

"Owing to the very critical position, all orders given to Irish Volunteers for tomorrow, Easter Sunday, are hereby rescinded, and no parades, marches or other movements of Irish Volunteers will take place. Each individual Volunteer will obey this order strictly in every particular."

The sisters were unaware that humanitarian activist, diplomat, poet and Irish Nationalist, Roger Casement, had landed in Kerry. Roger Casement was waiting for the German liner named *'The Aud'* which was to accompany Casement's submarine. The ship carried 20,000 rifles, millions of rounds of ammunition, machine guns and explosives. Alas, it had been stopped by a British patrol boat near Tralee. The news of Casement's arrest and the loss of the cargo of arms had reached the Volunteers' headquarters. It was to be believed that it was Casement who, at the last moment, got an appeal through to abandon the project. Casement and those who were with him were identified, captured and were shipped over to London.

Eoin MacNeill sent a Countermanding Order to be delivered to Volunteers throughout the country. The manoeuvres arranged for Easter Sunday were abandoned and the Rising appeared to be off. Chrissie did not sleep that night and would not sleep for many nights to come.

On Easter Monday, 26th April, 1916, the Dublin Battalion paraded, bearing arms and carrying one day's rations. Shortly after noon the GPO, the Four Courts, three railway termini and other important points circling the centre of Dublin were rushed and occupied.

At home in Red Cow Lane, the family was getting ready for a stroll when word got out. Chrissie knew Michael was at the GPO. She knew in her bones and soul he was there. Her face paled and her lips trembled, while her mother cursed the atheists and called them cowards.

Chrissie and Maggie ran towards the GPO. Both were surprised by the large gathering of Dubliners. Chrissie looked up to the windows scanning the faces, and with pride she raised her right hand and waved at the Volunteers who were looking out the window of the GPO. Chrissie hoped one was Michael. A woman passing by glared at Chrissie and Maggie and shouted, "How dare you wave to those cowards!" Both linked arms and carried on walking.

Suddenly the door at the GPO was opened and there stood poet and Irish rebel, Padraig Pearse. Maggie said, "He is saying something I cannot hear? Can you?" Chrissie was looking at the tricolour that was being raised, followed by an emerald green flag with gold writing on it.

Maggie shouted, "God, Chrissie, did I have sore fingers helping to sew those flags but Jeysus it was worth it, just to see this glorious moment." Chrissie kissed and hugged Maggie.

Circle of Fire and Steel

Many Martyrs were made in Ireland because of Pearse's 1915 'Bloodshed speech'. In the long queue of young martyrs was Michael. He was not prepared to accept Ireland's way of life under British rule like his parents and grandparents did. However, these boys were also unprepared, they were no better than Eoin MacNeill. They were dreamers, knights of courtly love, and their lover was Ireland. A provisional government was established with Padraig Pearse as head and a hundred youths, ill armed, standing their ground against the might of the British Army!

'Cumann na mBn,' the Irish Women's Council, and their leader Countess Markievicz, marched side by side through the streets of Dublin. They occupied Park Street. Eamon De Valera took over 'Boland Mill,' Thomas MacDonagh was at 'Jacobs' and many snipers were hidden in the background.

Outside The GPO, just after midday, the Proclamation of the Irish Republic was read out by the leader of the Provisional Government of the Irish Republic, Padraig Pearse:

Irishmen and Irishwomen! In the name of God and of the

dead generations from which she received the old tradition of nationhood........

The Irish tricolour was unfurled alongside. The tricolour was the emerald green flag with the gold words 'Irish Republic' and then the workers' flag 'The Plough and Stars'. Many Dubliners were surprised by the Volunteers. They were even more surprised to see the tricolour above the GPO, fluttering in the early spring breeze. Maggie and Chrissie's hearts swelled with nationalism. Essie was home in bed, she had worked a night shift. Some members of the public were vocal and called the rebels' names.

Inside the GPO laughter, camaraderie, bonhomie, filled the room and songs were sung, until a tall, red headed man dished out orders and positions were filled by windows facing the river Liffey. The tall burly figure of Michael Collins, losing his temper because some volunteers brought alcohol in. He boomed, "The British said we were drunk in 98. Well, they will not accuse us of being drunk in 1916!" Then he threw the bottles of beer away.

Most of the British Officer Corps were at the Curragh Races. The remaining British soldiers were in a relaxed mood like most of Dublin on this warm bank holiday Monday. Outside and on the street below were angry 'shawlies,' women waiting for their bit of pension from their husbands, who they recently waved off to fight a war in another man's land. They joined up out of desperation, they needed the money and the money came home through a pension in the GPO. Many of these men died for Britain and were buried in unmarked graves, at Flanders or Ypres.

Inside the GPO, Tim turned to Michael and shouted, "Feck, I have never seen so many women angry."

"Shit, duck, that fecking brick just missed me, whose side are you on, Missus?" Sean yelled out the window.

"Not yours, yea little gob shite, I want me man's money and I will have it. You fecker, go and fight a real war," screamed the woman with no teeth, and who looked about ninety.

The boys had not bargained for this. Michael remembered the 'Lockout' when the majority of the older folks were on the side of the church, and the church were on the side of the rich business men. He felt despondent, an anger rose within him. He wanted to shoot the woman dead, he aimed but did not fire. The only fire was in his belly.

The following morning, at 4 am, a British force of 4,500 men with artillery attacked the rebel strongholds and secured the Castle. The British army had to fight their way out of Mount

Street, the canal was covered by a Volunteer Force and in corner houses ferocious battles ensued. Michael and others saw the British army marching with their military might. Michael trembled he had never seen so many soldiers. He looked around him and saw no fear. Bravado kicked in and he thought, *This is where the real fighting begins.*

Essie had just finished her night shift, when they heard the noise. They went outside and saw the air thick with smoke and then the many barricades. Essie had decided while on her nursing shift, if the situation becomes serious, she would help. Outside and into the war zone she followed others into the GPO.

Tuesday morning at 5.30 am, Mary was up along with her two daughters, Essie was on a night shift. The two boys were stirring upstairs. The three knew that the huge booming sound that made the walls of Red Cow Lane shake was the British retaliating.

Chrissie paled, Maggie trembled. Mary grabbed her rosary beads and whispered, "Essie is due home soon." Chrissie and Maggie opened the back door and walked across the yard, the stench of burning and cordite hung in the air. Then Maggie opened the yard gate and noticed a lot of Army vehicles. Chrissie joined her sister, both jumped when they heard a "crack, crack" noise and the sound of metal studs hitting pavement. It was British troops running after Irish rebels. The sisters stood rooted to the spot, shaking and in shock. Maggie felt sick and then vomited at the yard entrance. Chrissie stood pale and muted as Maggie continued to vomit.

As she looked up Maggie saw many dead civilians who were shot by British soldiers in cold blood! Fear rose in Chrissie, she looked to her little sister and cried, " What if the Brits find out about me and Michael's relationship? God, I have now brought danger to the family!" Maggie grabbed her sister by the wrists and yelled, "Chrissie, shut up, shut up and let's get inside!"

Maggie ran past her mother up to the bedroom she shared with her mammy and sisters, acid burnt the inside of her mouth. She looked out of the window towards Dublin Town. Chrissie gushed out her words to her mother. "Mammy, Brits are everywhere!" Mary stared at her eldest daughter and thought of Michael Morrissey. He had not been around for a while. She pulled at her rosary beads. James sat by the fireside rocking back and forth, the battle noise, and his sisters being home, disturbed him. Christy and Alec were coming from the stables where they had been reassuring the horses.

Mary looked to the clock and realised Essie was not home and with a dried throat she spoke, "Essie is late, she should be home by now." The three women stared at each other open mouthed.

Inside the GPO the shelling was intense and there was no let up. The rebels' will was still intact and they were heroic in their fighting, but the GPO was now in grave danger. Essie tended to a thin young man with light grey eyes and fine strawberry blond hair. Essie knew he was dying. She held his hand as he called his mother. She watched his contorted face change to that of a young peaceful child.

She drew near to his ear and hummed the Irish lullaby 'Sleep, my child.' "Sleep peacefully, my child, sleep peacefully." She hoped he heard her among the screaming, gun fire, and cannon sounds. He smiled at her then let out a sigh. Essie closed his light grey eyes, wiped her hands in her uniform, sipped some cold tea and moved onto a red haired youth with green eyes. His chest ripped open as he gurgled for breath. She was surrounded by chaos, heat, blood and fear but still she remained calm.

Teresa Murray

Tuesday 25th April at 2pm, twenty-four hours after the rising, Sarah Murray was standing outside her own front door, Foley Street, Corporation buildings. Sarah was holding her youngest child Teresa in her arms. Her daughter played with the stray strands of hair from her mother's bun. The spring air avoided the tenements, there was only the stench of blood, smoke, shit and poverty. The rubbish danced, and swirled about in the wind. Sarah was shouting to her son who was in the yard. She demanded he came in away from out of the danger, the danger of snipers.

Sarah looked up to the blue sterile sky, suddenly she heard a whistling sound, and felt a sharp pain in her hand. Her little girl, Teresa, slumped forward onto her mother's breast. Sarah's hand felt something wet, she looked and saw blood. She noticed how quickly her daughter's colour had changed. She screamed, "Oh my God, Jesus Christ, no!!!"

Sarah's mind raced towards insanity, her heart thumped in her chest, bile rose in her throat. She ran towards the North Union building for the poor carrying her youngest child close to her. She stopped, looked down, saw her daughter gurgling on her own blood. Sarah fell to her knees, and howled her pain to the cloudless sky. The echoing tin, tin sound of shoe studs entered the air. Joseph, her husband, was running behind, he breathlessly caught up with his wife and child. He grabbed his wife and saw his youngest daughter and wept. Sarah howled into the hollow part of her husband's shoulder. Both cradled one another, while their daughter lay lifeless.

The Caffery house was on a knife edge, battle raged outside, no sign of Essie! Mary sat at the kitchen table, kale, onions and carrots left in a bowl untouched. James began to feel agitated by the noise and the commotion and cried, Mary heard nothing. Chrissie reassured her eldest brother the storm will pass. Mary murmured, *Hail Mary*, to herself, her lips moved quickly, but her hands stayed still. Maggie took the vegetables and began to peel, slice and cut. James sat by the peat fire and watched in agitation.

Wednesday, the British gunboat, the 'Helga,' sailed up the river Liffy. Michael and others rubbed their sleepy, red rimmed eyes. "Feck, a gunboat?" It aimed and fired at the Liberty Hall, then the GPO. Masonry filled the centre of Dublin creating a fog, then flames licked the fog away revealing horrific reality.

The Caffery house shuddered! All were under the table trembling. James screamed, "Mammy, is this the end of the world?" Maggie, with a laugh in her voice, showed no fear, "James, it is only thunder, God is angry." Mary, on her knees, thought of Essie and she prayed. The family were imprisoned in their own home, they had enough food, so no one went hungry. Yet, no member of the Caffery household had any appetite.

Mary began to scrub the table, beads of sweat laced her brow. Alec and Christy went to the stables and stayed there and prayed. The air was thick with fear. Chrissie could not take any more, she bypassed her mother and fled upstairs to the bedroom. She looked out of the window hoping to see Michael or Essie. Chrissie continued to look out of the window, she watched people scurry and rushing about, and coming and going from the pub. Some were shamelessly looting. She could see Dublin was now ablaze, an orange inferno. She said out loud, "This is Britain's revenge!"

"Christina!" She turned around, her mother was standing in the doorway. Both wept and held onto each other.

That evening, at supper time, Mary's face was flushed with emotion, her hands shook as she laid the table. She tried to say grace, no words came. She and her five children sat in silence. Essie was still not home. Suddenly there was a loud bang at the door which made everyone jump. Mary stood stoically, her arm outstretched, and ordered her children to stay where they were. Mary quickly opened the door, and there, before her, stood a broken man. It was her youngest brother, Joseph. He stood head down and kept repeating, "She's gone she's gone."

Mary froze and thought, *Who is gone, not Essie!* She blurted out, "Come in, Joe, sit down."

Her brother sat down, his head in his hands, and sobbed, "Teresa's gone, Mary, she was shot in the back."

Maggie dropped the kettle. James, sensitive by nature, cried out. Mary thought someone had hit her, and her stomach wretched, and she thought, *Did he say Teresa?* She reached out her hand to her brother and comforted him. Chrissie ran to James and took him out of the kitchen. Maggie, Alec and Christy stood open mouthed. Maggie thought *God this is hell on earth. I wish Essie came home. I wish all this never happened!*

Chrissie sat with James, tears streaming down her face. James looked to his sister, "Chrissie, why you crying?" She wiped her face in her cardigan sleeve and tried to block out the raging battle sounds and the cries and sobs that were coming from the kitchen.

Joseph stared ahead and spoke quietly, "Sarah was holding Teresa in her arms when a bullet grazed her hand and made it...." He stopped to let a sob out. Mary soothed her brother. He gulped, "Teresa was shot in the back...."

Mary wiped her face with the back of her hand, and shouted, "Who shot her Joe, who was it?"

Joseph Murray shook his head. "There was gun conflict with rebels and the Brits.... could be a stray bullet from a sniper or from a British soldier? I do not know...."

Mary whispered "Joe, Essie was on a night shift, she has not come home. I am worried sick."

Joe looked bewildered, coughed and wiped his face and spoke, "Mary, some nurses have gone into the GPO." Mary held her breath, clutched her brothers arm. Maggie held onto her mother's shoulders.

The family spent the next few days on a see-saw of emotions, sometimes Chrissie thought she would lose her mind with worry. The family were scared, and the stench and noise terrified them. Sometimes the sisters were brave enough to look out the bedroom window onto Dublin town. The landscape was dotted with skeleton buildings, ash and the smell of cordite hung in the air, mixed with human flesh.

The family gathered round the table in shock, grief and fear. However, the boys and Maggie put their fears aside and remained strong for their mother and elder sister. Alec got up and looked out the kitchen window, then opened the back door and shouted, "My God, Dublin is on fire!" The family, too scared to venture into the yard, stood in the door way.

The noise was deafening, the smell of burnt flesh and wood hung in the air, and it was difficult to breathe. James cried in agitation, "The sky is on fire." Mary took her vulnerable son back into the safety of their house. Maggie and her siblings looked out to Dublin city centre. They could see Nelson Column was lit up by the surrounding fire. Chrissie's heart was frozen in fear, fear for Michael's safety and her family's too.

By Thursday the British circle of fire and steel pressed closer to the central scene of operations. Every inch was contested by snipers and small bodies of desperate men. Michael Morrissey and his brother Liam were desperate men.

Friday, The O'Rahilly and his men left Moore Street to find safer headquarters. The O'Rahilly did not make it, he lay in a back lane for nineteen hours and, before he died, he wrote a love note to his wife. The British would not allow an ambulance to take this brave Celtic warrior.

Connolly and Pearse decided the wounded and nurses had to leave. Only Elizabeth O'Farrell, Julie Grenan and

Connolly's personal secretary, Winifred Carney, stayed. Essie, worn out with only snatches of sleep, reluctantly left with the others. Outside, the night air took her breath away, she felt faint. Her nursing friend Molly saw her colour drain and persuaded Essie to go home. The British saw the nurses and wounded leave and held their weapons. The wounded were taken to people's homes and other hospitals.

At Red Cow Lane, the small gate was opened and in walked Essie. Mary fell on her knees. Maggie screamed, "Essie my God, Essie!" Chrissie, Maggie, Alec and Christy ran to Essie, the four surrounded her. The five were crying, then they realised their mother was in the yard, sobbing. James rocked back and fore in the kitchen backdoor way.

Later, Essie, holding Chrissie's hand, spoke, "MacDonagh and the Irish rebels are trying to take over Jacobs, and are in armed conflict with Irish civilians. There's clubbing and shooting of civilians too."

"Essie, my job is meaningless to me. Michael matters more."

At the GPO was the rebels' commander, Johnny O'Hara, a tall broad shouldered man with a mop of strawberry blond hair, who liked a laugh and would often share a joke with the boys, but the boys knew when to draw the line and to not step over that line. He spoke, "Men, we will have to manoeuvre out from the building, and the only way out is the roof. A few of our boys are out there in their role as snipers, but do not rely on them, rely on yourselves and your own instincts."

The Irish volunteers were hot, dirty and very thirsty, yet they showed tremendous bravado. Then a piercing shrieking sound bounced off the walls. A piece of splinted wood split Tim's head in two and part of his brain was on the tiled floor. It left a grisly pattern of white, deep crimson and red. Michael and Sean ran to him and knelt down to comfort their friend. Michael felt Tim's dying breath on his cheek; his childhood friends and comrades witnessed his life ebb away.

Sean and Michael looked at each other and realisation hit them. Their bravado had been replaced by vulnerability. Sean wept, his tears revealed streaks of pale skin on his soot sodden face. Michael looked to his friend. "Not now, Sean, not now, God, don't give up, not now, take my hand and let's go out blazing."

Sean stood rooted in shock and fear. He looked to where Tim was lying and saw his childhood friend surrounded in his life's blood. Sean's mind raced and he shouted, "Is this what it was all for, is this what it is all about?!" He let go of his friend's hand, and ran the other way down the blazing stairs out through the door towards the barricades with his rifle in his arms. He aimed and fired.

As Sean fell, the horse chestnut tree in Phoenix Park came to his mind. He climbed to the top of the tree, he shook the branches. The conkers dropped down to the grass below, he looked down. Tim was waiting for him at the bottom. "Come on, it's time," he shouted. Sean floated down to his friend.

That night the sky over Dublin was shrouded in a crimson smoke, while rifles, machine guns and cannons boomed and clattered into the air. The rebel lines were being broken. The British Army concentrated on the headquarters, the GPO, and where the Republican flag flew.

Horrific bombardment set the centre of Dublin ablaze, banks, churches and business places were aflame and tottering. Dublin was broken and many innocent people died. The GPO's flames licked away the dying embers of the rebels' cause as ash floated over Dublin.

Saturday, 29th April, in a two up two down terrace house in Moore Street and the new headquarters of the Volunteer Army, James Connolly lay badly wounded. Pearse wrote his

first manifesto. Pearse read out, *"I desire now......................*
For my part as to anything I have done in this, I am not
afraid to face either judgment or posterity."

Saturday, 29th April, Pearse had ordered all volunteers to lay
down arms. In the afternoon, Pearse sent a message with a
nurse Elizabeth O'Farrell asking for terms, the terms were
refused. Nurse Elizabeth O'Farrell left the new headquarters
at Moore Street and walked towards the British waving a
white handkerchief. The very brave Elizabeth walked to
every rebel hold waving her white handkerchief. At 2pm
Pearse surrendered to the British Army along with James
Connolly, Thomas Clarke, Joseph Plunkett, Sean Mac
Dermott, and Michael Collins. The Dublin Rising gave
Ireland its blood sacrifice!

Christy and Alec were in the yard looking out onto Dublin
Town when the gate to the yard banged open, both boys
jumped. They saw Mrs Kenny, she was fuming, the colour of
her face matched her red hair. She knocked the door. Mary
jumped up and opened the door. She looked above her
neighbour's head, and saw smoke billowing over Dublin's
centre. Mrs Kenny was angry and vocal, "The GPO been
taken over by a band of rebels. I could not believe it, it is bad

enough losing my husband. How am I to feed my banes, the injustice of it all?"

Mary's heart had missed a beat, she felt the anger rise in her belly.

"Sorry, Mrs Caffery, are you all right, your colour has changed."

"Oh I am fine, grand, well, not grand about the shenanigans of our own stopping the widows from getting their money. Mrs Kenny, if you do not mind, I must get on." Mary took her rosary out and began to pray for all, except Michael Morrissey.

Days seemed to be filled with horror stories and gossip. Chrissie was so terrified she was on the edge of madness. Saturday evening the family sat down to supper, suddenly Alec looked up, "Did you hear something then?" He gingerly walked over to the window that looked out on to the yard; he saw a head looking over the top of the gate. "Mammy, out the lamp, there is someone trying to get into the yard."

The room was in darkness, no one spoke, the only sound was a snuffling noise from Chrissie. Alec looked out again, he recognised the person, it was his friend Frankie McGuire. "It's all right, it is Frankie." He opened the back door, the horses did not sense the stranger, they were too agitated and highly strung from the bombing, gun firing and screams that came from Dublin Town. The constant snorting and stamping of hooves echoed throughout the yard.

Alec tiptoed across the yard, said words of comfort to the horses and went over to his friend. "Alec, I have news for Chrissie, Michael's been captured he has been taken to Richmond Barracks, that's all I can say. I have got to go, keep the faith, Alec."

Alec said nothing, he turned round and walked towards the homely glow that was coming from the kitchen. Alec looked to his mother, who stood in the door way and gulped, "Michael has not been killed, Chrissie." Chrissie let out a cry of relief, her sisters comforted her. Mary looked to her second eldest son, she knew it was not good news. "He has been captured and is interned at Richmond Barracks." Chrissie held her head in her hands and sobbed while her family looked on helplessly.

The three sisters shared the same lumpy bed, Chrissie, groggy through lack of sleep and heartache, pushed Maggie awake, Essie was soft with sleep. Maggie, through her sleepy eyes, saw her sister's beautiful face shrouded in grief. "Maggie, please come with me to Richmond Barracks, I might see Michael." Maggie nodded yes.

That evening both sisters walked to Richmond Barracks. The evening air smelt good, it had a frost tinge to it. On reaching the barracks both were stunned. It was like a funeral, wives sobbed, lovers cried, and men looked on bewildered. Inside the barracks, Michael was totally oblivious, he lay on his bed and stared into space.

Thursday, May 3rd, was the day of Teresa's funeral. The room was bare, except for the small white coffin that Dublin Union paid for. The coffin sat on a square table. A small group of family and mourners huddled in the corner. Joseph gingerly walked to the coffin that contained his precious daughter, he kissed the top of the lid. Sarah rocked back and forth and wailed her pain. Mary held her sister-in-law in her arms. Sarah's tears soaked the shoulder of Mary's dress.

Joseph carefully picked up the coffin of his two-year-old daughter, Teresa. He stumbled out the door and stopped for a brief moment. He then walked alone to Glasnevin cemetery to bury his daughter in an unmarked grave.

Sarah was calmed by Mary. She looked to her sister-in-law, squeezed her hand and sighed, stared at the damp patch on the wall and said, "I wished the bullet took me instead of Teresa. Seven children were killed that afternoon, in and around this area and my little girl was the youngest

96

aged 28 months."

Mary arrived home emotionally exhausted, her daughters were preparing the evening meal. Mary noticed Chrissie wipe a stray tear. Then Chrissie cried, "Oh mammy, Padraic Pearse, Thomas MacDonagh and Tom Clarke were shot by the British." Mary was shocked and felt dizzy, her daughter caught her before she fell.

Sixteen were executed after the Easter Uprising of 1916. Patrick Pearse, Joseph Mary Plunkett, Michael O'Hanrahan, Michael Mallin, Sean MacDermott, Roger Casement, Thomas J Clarke, Edward Ned Daly, John MacBride, Cornelius Colbert, James Connolly, Thomas MacDonagh, William Pearse, Eamonn Ceannt, Sean Heuston, Thomas Kent. All died for the cause.

The execution of the sixteen rebels left a bitter taste in Ireland's mouth. It had a dramatic affect on Mary. She never referred to Michael Morrissey as an atheist again, he was a hero. Chrissie and Maggie made the trip to Richmond Barracks every day, hoping to see Michael. Then Michael was shipped out to Britain, to a jail in Stafford, from there onto Frongoch, North Wales.

Many thought it was sheer madness, a few ill armed

youths threw down a gage to an Empire. Yet, had the 'Aud' safely landed its cargo, followed by further consignments then a certain area of the country could have been captured, entrenched and held for an indefinite period. Some 100,00 men could have secured the fighting line. The British Army would have been crushed facing such a magnitude, supported by German air and navy attacks on the English coast, and submarine bases in ports seized by rebels. England would have needed practically to withdraw her forces from the Western Front!

However, the Easter Monday Rising had no such military prospects of success. The British Army were in shock, caught off guard and to prevent being caught off guard again! They turned on their own and beat Ireland senseless!

Yet, the British could not control Irish thoughts, hearts and the memories of Easter, 1916. The anger, injustice, the killing of the sixteen came out in sores and seeped into the young and came out in 1919.

A year later, May 12th 1917, a warm spring day, Chrissie and Maggie raced towards the Liberty Hall, the building that gave birth to the Union and 'The Citizen Army,' and now a soup kitchen and bomb factory. Breathlessly, the sisters wormed their way through the heaving throng and stood at the front of the crowd. Both saw a ton of coal and nails barricading the main entrance to the Liberty Hall. Above was a white linen banner displaying the words 'The anniversary of James Connolly's murder, May 12th, 1916,' on either side fluttering was the tricolour. Both sisters stood in awe at this rebellious yet very moving event. Maggie nudged Chrissie, "Here's the police."

The crowd began to boo and jeer, so did the sisters. The police requested that the banner be taken down, their request was refused. The police had no option but to get a ladder from the fire service and climb to the banner and take it down. "Boo," cried Chrissie and others.

Then Maggie let out a belly laugh and elbowed Chrissie and shouted, "Look Chrissie, another banner." Four women inside the Liberty Hall had climbed to the roof and were waiting with another banner that was unfurled.

Chrissie shouted, "One of those women is Ireland's own rebel, Rosie Hackett."

On their return journey home, Chrissie, with a laugh in her voice, said, "Maggie, can you believe it, four hundred police to restrain four women."

Maggie replied, "And no arrest, those women did wonders for the police's reputation, ha ha."

The following day Chrissie told Maggie that Rosie Hackett said the reason there was no arrest was because four women arrested by four hundred police officers would not look good in the press.

"Christina, are you demonstrating again?"

"Mammy, this time it is different, John Dillon has walked out on the English government in support of Sinn Féin, and not only that, the church is behind us on this occasion. They denounced conscription as oppressive and inhumane."

Christy looked bewildered at his oldest sister, "Chrissie what is oppressive?"

"Ah Christy, oppressive is this English government that will not leave Ireland alone, and now wants to force our boys and girls into fighting England's war."

James looked at his sister and brother. "Does this mean that I have to fight?"

"No, no, James, no one is going to any war. Ireland is united on this."

Mary looked sternly at Chrissie. "Be careful on this march."

Maggie and Chrissie were making their way to the centre of

Dublin, to a mass rally. Chrissie turned to Maggie. "Oh, Maggie, I have never seen Michael so happy, it is grand that the church has spoken out too. He says this could be a turning point for Ireland, and I think so too." Maggie nodded and smiled. She noticed the size of the crowd, the banners waving and she sang along to the protest songs. She felt joy, joy and pride to be taking part and doing her bit for Ireland.

No one expected the war to last long and many young men joined. Joined up for the money, they did not think of death, only putting food into their very hungry families' bellies.

The Robber of Youth, 1919

Essie was in between Chrissie and Maggie, she was a delicate baby who grew in to a fine boned but sickly child. Sickly children seem to grow and retain an air of delicate beauty, making their eyes larger than normal, adding more translucent beauty, almost saint like. Essie had a very caring nature and this took her into nursing. She was a shy daydreamer and her family meant everything to her.

The sun was just reaching the yard wall when Mary saw the gate open. Her fragile daughter, Essie, stumbled towards the kitchen door. Mary opened the door letting in her daughter and the cold February air. "Mammy my throat is sore, it feels like I have swallowed a bag of rusty nails".

"Essie you were fine this morning at breakfast."

"I feel so tired, I need to lie down."

Essie was so weak her mother Mary undressed her and put her to bed. Not the bed she shared with her two sisters but Mary's own lumpy bed. Mary went downstairs and made a punch, using hot water, sugar and a little whiskey. Upstairs Essie could not lift her head off the pillow and her chest was heavy, she rolled her tongue around her mouth, it had a metallic taste. She felt something trickle from her mouth, she wiped it with the back of her hand and saw her own blood, dark blood. From her nursing experience she knew this was a bad sign.

Mary returned to the bedroom and quietly entered the room, Essie looked anaemic, yet angelic. Essie's chestnut brown hair spread on the pillow that had seen better days. Essie, through gasps, told her mother to isolate her from the rest of the family, "Just you look after me, Mammy."

Mary stood, her hand over her mouth and watched her pale, thin, fragile daughter gasp for breath, saw the blood flow from her daughter's mouth. Mary sobbed, "Oh God, Pthisis." (Pulmonary tuberculosis.) Mary was frantic. She ran down the stairs out into the bone cold yard. Alec had just returned. She shouted to Alec, "Fetch the doctor, it is Essie!" Mary ran back up the stairs and knelt on the floor, her head bowed on the bed with Essie's hand in hers. She cried, "Come on, Essie, darling, stay with us."

Breathlessly, Alec stood in the doorway. Mary raised her hand and, in hushed tones, she said, "Stay out." Alec saw his sister and he stammered, "No doctor, the hospital is full of soldiers ill with Spanish flu."

Mary, through a veil of tears, sobbed, "Alec, get the family home please, get them now." Mary wiped her daughter's sweating body then laid her down and tilted the cup to her mouth, it was no use. Essie had stopped swallowing. Mary's heart raced as she prayed for her daughter to live. Sun cast its shadow on the back bedroom wall, creating shapes. Mary drew the curtains and an amber glow surrounded her and Essie.

Downstairs James was lost and forgotten, he became agitated and shouted, "Mammy, why are you upstairs?!"

Mary sat helplessly as Essie shivered, then sweated and became delirious. Essie's breathing became shallow and her chest made a rattling sound. Alarmed, Mary sobbed, "We need to get the priest now!"

Lying on her back, Essie looked into her mind's eye. She heard whispering and saw the sea at Sandymount. She held Christy's hand, she felt the sand between her toes. Chrissie, Maggie and Alec were up ahead, her mother and James were behind. She heard a seagull and watched it dive into the sea. Essie and Christy ran to catch up with the others.

Essie heard a clip clop of horse's hoofs on cobble stones, she could smell the mustiness of the four legged beast. She sat on the front of the cart and looked up to the sky that was a blanket of blue, not a cloud to be seen. The cart slowly moved and the horse swished its tale. She looked to the side, she noticed her father's hands were on the reins, ingrained in dirt and prominent green blue veins stood out. He turned to Essie and smiled, she smiled back. They both looked behind and waved to her mother, Chrissie, Maggie, James, Alec and little Christy. Essie began to moan. Then a tear fell down her pale angelic cheek. Mary began to cry, " Essie, Essie."

Essie and her father looked to each other and her father said. "Let's go." They turned, smiled and waved goodbye.

Father O'Reilly entered the candlelit room, saw Mary's arched back, her hands holding her daughter's cold, pale hand. The priest knew Essie was dead. He tapped Mary on the shoulder. Mary fell to the floor and wailed. The two boys stood in shock and disbelief. Downstairs, James paced the floor and cried for his mother. Alec and Christie cried for their beautiful sister, Essie. Maggie and Chrissie both stumbled up the stairs. They heard their mother's cries. They pushed the door open and bumped into Father O'Reilly who had tears in his eyes too.

On the bedside table the priest placed his white linen cloth and a glass jug filled with holy water. The priest continued with the ritual of the last rights to the frail twenty-one-year-old. While her mother and siblings sobbed, Maggie opened the window to release Essie's spirit. The busy sound of Smithfield market filled the room along with a fresh, winter breeze. Christy looked out over the roof tops and heard a robin sing its beautiful tune. He thought, *How can that bird sing at a time like this, when Essie is not here to listen to this beautiful bird song.*

Mary, all in black, was held up by her two sons, Alec and Christy. Michael was in the middle of Chrissie and Maggie, holding their hands. Behind was Mary's brother Joseph, Sarah and James Boyce, other families and friends. All followed the coffin that was on the family horse and cart surrounded in winter flowers, Frankie McGuire at the reins. James was at home with Mrs Kenny who was also helping to arrange the food. James asked Mrs Kenny, "What are we celebrating with all this food?" Mrs Kenny, sighed, "We are celebrating a life, James." He sighed, "Ah, I like that."

Essie died, aged twenty one, on a cold winter's day in February, 1919, from what was then romantically known as 'The Robber of Youth', Phthisis, TB. In the middle of the twentieth century, they discovered that tuberculosis was transmitted by inhalation of contaminated droplets. Essie was a nurse, and nursing during the time when the 'Spanish flu' invaded the world.

Wales

1899 to 1919

In May 1831, the industrial town of Merthyr rose and shouted, "Caws and Bara" (Cheese and Bread). They were protesting over poor wages and high unemployment. The protest spread through villages and valleys. The Bad Debtors court was sacked and the goods that had been collected along with the account books, containing debtors' details, were destroyed. On June 1st the British Government ordered the Army to be dispatched to Merthyr. They were ordered to protect essential buildings and people. The working class held their own and the red flag of Socialism was ablaze. Yet, the army won and many of the working class were sent to the other side of the world. Innocent Richard Lewis, known as Dic Penderyn, was arrested and found guilty of a crime he never committed and was hung at 8am on 13th August at the gallows at St Mary's Street, Cardiff. The British Government wanted at least one rebel as an example so they hung an innocent man, aged twenty three, married and a father.

1839 - 1843, the Rebecca Riots took part in rural West Wales, Pembrokeshire, Carmarthenshire and Cardiganshire. A series of protests were made by tenant farmers against payment of tolls (fees charged to use the roads). There were big social divisions between land holders and the small tenant farmers and labourers who worked the land. The gentry tended to belong to the Anglican Church

(Church of England), spoke English, and they often served as local magistrates or poor law officers who fixed the poor rate, the tolls and tithes. They had little in common with those who worked the land. The rest of the population was Welsh speaking and non conformist. During the riots, men disguised as women, called themselves 'Rebecca and her Daughters.' They took their name from the bible. (Rebecca talks of the need to possess the gates of those who hate them.) The authorities eventually suppressed the Rebecca rioters using troops and the law.

IIn 1899, Wales was on the crest of an industrial revolutionary wave. This ocean of industry was soaked in copper from Swansea to Anglesey. The hinterland, the Welsh Valleys, was alive with people and coal. Wales was a world monopoly, directed by the rise of the massive iron, steel, coal, later tinplate industries. The country's labour fertilised whole tracts of the world from Pennsylvania to the Donetz basin. Wales was a critical factor in the world's economic development. South Wales merchants bought shipping companies from French ports and Hamburg. Italy, Argentina, Brazil worked to the rhythms of South Wales's trade.

Despite all this Wales lay in the arms of the booming sounds of the industrial revolution and fell asleep. There was

*no one out there to nurture, to guide or fight for an
independent Wales! There were Welshmen like Mardy, born
Arthur Horner, who was in James Connolly's Citizen Army
and was at the Easter Rising 1916. In South Wales, Saunders
Lewis formed 'The Welsh Movement' (Y Mudiad Cymreig)
and in North Wales, Huw Roberts Jones created 'The Welsh
Home Rule Army' (Byddin Ymreolwyr Cymru). Saunders
Lewis and Huw Roberts Jones came together and from this
The National Party of Wales (Plaid Genedlaethol Cymru)
was born but born too late! They met in secret in Penarth, on
the outskirts of Cardiff where party business was conducted
in Welsh, and at a time when the Welsh language was on the
decline. The National Party of Wales came into being on the
edge of 'The Depression' and God help Wales!*

*During the time of the Easter Rising, Cardiff MP, Ivor Guest,
became the last Lord Lieutenant of Ireland .*

*In the early nineteenth century, Cardiff was still a small
town, largely untouched by the Industrial Revolution. In 1839
it developed into a major port, with the first stage of the Bute
Dock. Cardiff's harbour faced south and its proximity to the
sea, with its natural harbour, made it an ideal site for
development, and the extension of the Taff Railway line. This*

gave the coal fields of the South Wales Valleys a direct route to the sea. The first train load of Rhondda steam coal, reached Cardiff on December 17th, 1855. By the 1890s Cardiff was Britain's largest coal exporting port. Along with Cardiff Docks, there was the Dowlais Steel Works, which was at East Moor in 1891.

A flat piece of land, on the outskirts of Cardiff, known as East Moors, was an area called Splott. The name Splott came from the English, the English who came from the West Country to work the farm fields of St Mellons and the Vale of Glamorgan, replacing Welsh farm workers who left the land for the valleys and coal.

The people from the West Country, Somerset, Devon, Cornwall often used the letter S at the beginning of words, a plot of land on the outskirts of East Moors became Splott. They were pickers of fruit and were joined by many Irish who came because the money was good. The English and Irish would later work the docks of Newport, Cardiff, Penarth and Barry. During the Famine of 1846 a lot of Irish left Ireland. However, some were enticed to leave by the likes of the Marquess of Bute to become underpaid labourers at the new docks.

In 1899, William Griffin aged twenty seven did not work with coal, steel, tinplate, or as a farm labourer, he was a journeyman painter and decorator. He lived at number 65, Adeline Street, Splott, and was a widower, his first wife Clara Croden was Irish. Within two years of their marriage his wife sadly died, leaving him childless. Twenty doors down at number 83 lived William and Ann Evans. William Evans's family left Carmarthen during the Rebecca Riots. They ran away instead of being sent away to the other side of the world. The Evans family left the land and healthy living for a life of uncertainty in the area around St John's Church, a poverty stricken area in the middle of the town of Cardiff.

Their daughter, Charlotte, was a young carefree, single twenty-year-old. She was unaware that she caught the eye of the young handsome widower and journeyman painter and decorator. William was striking to look at, with a head of thick auburn hair and bright blue laughing eyes. He was a charmer and women flocked to him. Charlotte worked at the local Ironmongers off Albany Road and her route to work took her past where William lived. Charlotte was totally oblivious to her good looking neighbour.

William stopped outside Davies's Ironmongers and Haberdashery, he tried to see his reflection, but all he saw was the shop's wares: buckets, spades and brushes hung from iron hooks that made a tinny sound in the breeze. William pushed open the big oak door, as he entered a bell chimed. He stood in front of the beech wooded oblong counter that ran the length of the shop. Behind the counter were rolls of material waiting to be unravelled. In front of him stood a petite young woman with jet black hair that would not look out of place on a Spanish Señorita. She smiled, and William noticed that she had a small gap between her two front teeth, and how her eyes sparkled. He was taken aback, he did not expect to see his attractive neighbour, who made his heart flutter, working in the shop. His thoughts flew around his head. *Could this be the moment for me to ask her to go courting?* He lost his cocky nerve, coughed and politely asked the young lady, "Is Mr. Davies in, please?" The girl spoke in a soft voice, "I will get him for you now, Sir."

William, who could normally talk a glass eye to sleep, was lost for words. He stood and played with the edge of his green tweed cap, trying not to stare at the raven haired beauty. Mr. Davies, a jolly, red-faced man with a shiny bald head and a big smile greeted William. "How are you doing, my friend?"

"Dan, I have the decorating contract for the ceilings at the new Civic Centre at Cathays Park."

"Well done, William, so what can I do for you?" His

113

friend said with a smile.

"I need some good paint, brushes and some methylated spirits, oh, and dust sheets. Do you have any old material that you cannot sell, that I can use?"

"Leave it with me William. Miss Evans will be going on her lunch break shortly. I will close the shop and see what I have got, and what needs ordering. Come back later, say 2 pm."

"Thank you Dan, you are a good friend."

William Griffin made his way towards the shop door and from the corner of his eye he saw Charlotte untie her apron from her slim body and put on a ruby red cardigan. She was off to Roath Park to have her lunch. She waved goodbye to her boss, Mr. Davies, and then closed the door. She walked into the late spring afternoon, and ignored the smells and the busy street.

"Hello, Miss Evans do you mind if I join you?" William found his voice and startled Charlotte. She nodded yes. They walked the busy pavement in silence, he noticed, for a short woman, she could walk fast, and he found it a struggle to keep up with her. William, a vain man who got by on his good looks, turned on the charm. His charm and good looks did not enthral Miss Evans. So he continued talking nervously to Charlotte. Charlotte thought to herself. *Who does he think he is, I hardly know him.*

She glanced at his moving hands and noticed he was not wearing a wedding ring. Charlotte spoke, "Do you ever stop talking? God help the woman that marries you."

William looked deeply into Charlotte's light grey eyes and said, "Play your cards right and you could be the next Mrs. Griffin." Charlotte glared. William liked this feisty woman. She was a challenge for him, a change from the dopey love struck women he had been attracting.

Charlotte continued to confidently walk ahead. At the park she sat on the first bench by the rose garden. The garden was heady with scent from the roses, the sound from the bees and the warm spring sunshine. She turned to William and said, "I am sitting here, you can join me if you want. I have two dripping sandwiches, would you like one?"

William declined, he was enticed by the challenge and stared at Charlotte. She was oblivious and continued to enjoy her sandwich. Suddenly she glanced up and said, "Why are you staring at me?" William's face flushed and he lit a cigarette while Charlotte ate.

Over time, William's natural charismatic personality finally won Charlotte's heart. November 18th, 1899 at Cardiff Register Office, Charlotte was a very unhappy, four months pregnant, bride. Her raven hair was worn in a large mass, with a bun on top, her suit was deep red and on her feet she wore button high black boots, in her hand there was a small posy of red roses. William looked handsome in his black suit, gold shirt studs and matching tie pin. Their two friends, Benjamin Hopkins and Ada Bonds, were witnesses.

William's mother, Elizabeth, was there with her third husband. She had been widowed twice. James Griffin, William's father, was her second husband, James came from the West of Ireland and one of the many impoverished families who were paid emigration money to get off the English landowner's land. James left Ireland as a young man and was a sailor when he met Elizabeth. Later he gave up the sea and became a Dock Gateman at Tiger Bay. Sadly, he died before his son William was born.

Charlotte's parents, William and Ann Evans, both dressed in their Sunday best. The quiet hard-working couple held a small reception in their front parlour where William dominated the afternoon with his charm and singing, while Charlotte looked on tight lipped.

William and Charlotte were married less than a year when the novelty had worn off. It was not long before good looking William was looking at other women. April, 1900, William was working in Barry, and living with another woman when his son Richard Charles was born.

Richard Charles, known as Dick, was born April 30th, 1900, in Adeline Street, Splott. Charlotte went on to have five more children in quick succession. Florence May, Doris, Victor, James and Charlotte Maude. Charlotte lived a life of controlled uncertainty. William was like the Scarlet Pimpernel, he turned up when he felt like it, totally unaware of his hungry children and downtrodden wife. After ten years of marriage to her womanising husband, Charlotte was worn out and her feistiness had long gone. Charlotte did not forgive but accepted her husband's behaviour for the sake of their children.

The family moved to bigger premises around the corner to 38, Railway Street, Splott. Railway Street was built in 1881, the street ran parallel to the railway line. The Splott area was a maze of houses, shops, taverns and it had a board school. The board school was in Dick's Street. At the end of the street, stood a large, Gothic style Catholic Church called 'St Albans on the Moor.' The Griffin family did not attend this church, religion had no significance for the family.

Dick's father William sometimes had to travel outside Cardiff for work and often left Charlotte alone for days with no money. Dick, the eldest child, witnessed the distress this caused his mother. He became distant from his father and more protective towards his mother. When not anxious about his mother, Dick would be allowed to be a child and would race to Splott Park and its cricket and football pitches and he loved swimming in the lido.

Sometimes they ventured out and crossed over the busy Newport Road to the posh park called Roath Park. The park had a large lake, and botanic gardens. You could hire boats, but Dick and his friends could not afford the boat rides so they spent many happy hours paddling in Roath Brook. However, when bored they would shout at passing boats. Sometimes they threw stones to make ripples on the lake. The young pranksters were soon stopped when the 'Parky' caught them and, if caught, he would give them a clip around the ear for their troubles.

Dick's siblings and his friends' favourite place, was playing on the docks. The dock area had a large Irish community. Later, people from North Africa, China and Europe came, bringing with them many spices and their different accents.

The community in the dock and surrounding area consisted of residential and commercial. However, this intended socially and economically mixed development was short lived. Sea captains, pilots, merchants and coal and steel owners moved out to the suburbs of Llandaff and the town of Penarth.

It was a wonderful, early summer's day. Dick, his brother Victor and their friends raced along the docks, passing fishing and sailing boats, and the pleasurable paddle steamers that blew smoke. The sound of industry and seagulls' cries filled the air. The nearer the boys got the more human sounds they could hear. The four had never seen so many posh people. Bunting was flying everywhere, everyone seemed happy.

The four friends weaved their way through the very large crowds. Dick's heart jumped when he saw the mast, it was decked out in colourful bunting. They were amazed by this wonderful sight. The four stood there open-mouthed, taking in the happy occasion. Harry, Dick's friend looked around, he noticed people looking at him and his bare feet. Harry's parents could not afford shoes, he went everywhere in bare feet. There were many children like Harry in Splott at the time.

The boy looked up to his judges, and poked his tongue out, the gentry looked down on him and his friends, in horror. One man, who wore a bowler hat, and who looked like 'King Edward' went to grab the boy. Dick saw this and kicked him with his hobnail boot, the man yelped. Dick responded, "You forgot, Mister, I am wearing boots."

The four friends ran and ducked and dived in among the crowd. They stopped to see the stern turn past Penarth Head, towards the Bristol Channel. The day was June 15th, 1910. The four friends witnessed Captain Scott's ship, 'The Terra Nova,' sail out from Cardiff docks on its British Antarctic Expedition. This historical event had no class, and everyone came out to bear witness. A day Dick and Harry would always remember.

During the summer, Dick and his friends would walk the four miles to the village of St Mellons, St Mellons was just outside Cardiff in Monmouthshire. Dick was up before the sun rose, up with the lark. Dick, his brother, Victor, Harry and two others walked the old Roman road and witnessed the sun rise over the Bristol Channel. The only other people about were the road cleaner, shovelling horse manure, and the milkman and his rattling milk cart. "How far, Dick?!" the four cried in unison.

Dick, all skin and bone, turned round and sighed. "When we see the 'Bluebell Inn,' we will stop to have some water and something to eat." In the distance the boys could see the rows of green farm fields, some of the fields were carpeted in colours of reds, blacks and yellow. They were filled with fruit that was ripe for picking. The sky was summer blue as the boys sat in the gutter, eating cold potatoes and swigging water from a bottle. All had scabbied knees and a tied marked necks. Dick lit a cigarette and stared ahead. His father had not come home last night and the image of his mother sat at the kitchen table, looking bereft, haunted Dick and made him angry. He would give his earnings from the fruit picking to his mother. Dick kicked Victor's boot. "Come on, kidder, let's go."

The farmer saw the boys slowly walking and shouted, "Come on, Lads, where have you been? The fruit be gone over ripe!" The farmer's wife, a large big busted woman, looked sternly at the boys while she gave them the empty baskets. They made their way to the sweet smelling chore. Dick thought, *We never eat fruit at home but we are not at home* and so he quickly gobbled a couple of strawberries.

Later, the farmer's wife would bring hard bread, with even harder cheese for the boys' lunch, along with home-made lemonade. The lemonade never touched the sides, straight down their dry thirsty throats. 5pm the bell rang to stop working. The boys stacked their baskets at the bottom of the farmer's wife's feet, and looked up at her rosy, unsmiling face, her arms folded across her huge breasts. Dick looked up at her bare arms. They reminded him of large slices of ham.

Money in their pockets, Dick and his friends walked the four miles back to Splott. Dick shouted as he ran past, "Easier going downhill, boys." As he ran his mind ached with apprehension and he wished his father would never come home, but he knew in his heart he would come home, and his suffering mother would forgive him. He looked at the five pennies in his hand and breathed in the fruit and copper.

He could see his mother smile in his mind's eye and this made him happy. Three miles in, East moor came into view and Splott Park with its outdoor swimming pool. The inviting view gave the boys renewed energy. They jumped into the ice cold water in their knitted underwear, their laughter bounced off the walls, and they laughed till their ribs were sore and their bellies ached for food.

The sun became an orange ball, a rolling light of heat that spread onto the rows of terraced houses. Dick ran down Railway Street, and pushed open the front door. Charlotte sat waiting, not for Dick, for William. His heart sank as he handed the money to his mam. She placed her hand upon his head, ran her fingers through his auburn hair and kissed his forehead. Dick was only happy when his mam was happy, and his mother was seldom happy.

Dick shouted, "Boys, we are off into town to see Willows' air ship."

"Airship?" The boys cried in unison.

"Yep, airship, you lot coming?"

The gang looked up open-mouthed. Dick walked off and then they quickly followed. Up the busy Newport Road and for devilment they dodged among the cars and trams. Once on the pavement they tried to race the cars. A horse and cart drew near, the boys shouted, "Boo," at the horse, the carter raised his fist and in return the boys poked their tongues out and laughed their way towards Cardiff Civic Centre.

At the Civic Centre there was a huge gathering of people and the Willows airship. The boys were amazed by the ship and were astounded by the small machine beneath it. They tried to get a better look, but the sound of gas being released made the boys jump so they stood back. The sausage-shaped machine lifted into the air and the boys whooped with excitement. For a couple of minutes the huge shadow of the airship blocked out the sun. Tilting their heads back as far as they could, they watched this magnificent machine fly over Cardiff.

Dick was a natural leader and a very popular boy in Railway

Street. The gang always hung outside his home. One time Harry and his friends stood outside Dick's house waiting for their leader to lead the day's adventure. Dick opened the front door, stepped onto the pavement, hops from 'Brains brewery' hung in the air. "Boys, fancy a walk to Pengam Green?"

"Pengam Green!" the boys replied in unison.

"All right, I will go on my own to see the first air flight over the Bristol Channel!" The gang stared and Dick said, "Follow me."

Breathlessly, they got to the top of the green to be greeted by a large crowd. Dick's hair fluffed up in the breeze, he surveyed the crowd, then suddenly it went quiet. They heard an unfamiliar sound. They saw the plane's shadow on the grass before they saw the plane. The boys watched in wide eyed amazement as it flew above their heads and over the Bristol Channel towards Western Super Mare. Everyone whooped with joy.

"Where is it going, Harry?" shouted Victor.

"England"

"England?"

"Yes, that is England over there."

On the way home, Dick spread his arms out wide, and he

made a whirring noise as he ran like the wind. "I prefer the plane to Willows airship, the airship looks like a big whale."

"Na, more like a large sausage," shouted Harry.

Dick stopped playing planes and said, "You knows we got a football team now?"

"Who?"

"We have."

"Who?"

"Cardiff."

"Cardiff?"

"Yes, Cardiff City Football Club and the football pitch is in Canton."

"Could we walk there?"

"No," they all shouted at Harry.

Victor rolled his shirt and began to use it as a football. His eldest brother and friends chased him. The boys giggled, twisted, turned and dived, covered in mud and leaving laughter on the wind.

June 28th, 1914, Archduke Ferdinand of Austria and his wife were assassinated in Sarajevo. A month later on July 28th, the First World War began.

Dick had left school, and was working as an apprentice

painter and decorator for Cardiff Corporation. Harry, his friend, worked as a labourer down the docks. Both friends looked at their favourite park, Splott Park, the four football pitches converted to agricultural fields because of the war. Dick was short and skinny for his age. Like a lot of children, he was undernourished, but undernourished because of his father's womanising ways. His mop of auburn hair, and large blue eyes distracted many from his thinness. However, there was always a cigarette in his mouth.

Harry was the same height with dark brown curly hair. Harry shared Dick's cigarette and blew out smoke as he spoke. "How come that Duke got a Spanish sounding name, like my boss Louie Ferdinand, when we all know he is Austrian?"

"Beats me," Dick replied.

"Do you think the war will last long?"

"Na, my father said it should be over by Christmas."

In 1916, conscription was brought in and it was not popular. 200,000 demonstrated against it in Trafalgar Square, and many failed to respond to the call-up. In the first year 1.1 million joined. Britain needed more men and, on March 2nd, 1916, conscription was brought in to force.

Dick and Harry often met up after work to play pitch and toss, and chat. "Did you hear about Russell Street, Dick? The Irish wants to call it Patriots' Row because of their men folk killed during the war."

Dick blew out his cigarette smoke. "I agree they're a bit cheeky in it like."

Harry replied, "I can't see Britain allowing the street to be renamed after the Easter Rising in Dublin can you?"

Dick stamped on his fag butt, put his hands in his pockets, sniffed the freshly turned soil from their old football pitch and said, "Na."

Dick was in the back yard polishing his boots, when he overheard his parents' conversation. William was washing his brushes as Charlotte prepared food. "Lottie, I see Belgian refugees have arrived at Cardiff Central."

"Yes, I know, William, I am worried, how long do you think the war will last?"

"Well, we got the big push now and with the Empire coming in as well, a couple of months, maybe."

"Well, I hope it finishes before Richard is eighteen."

Dick coughed and his parents looked up. His father said, "All right, Kidder?"

"Yep," Dick gulped.

In March 1918, Dick came home from work soaking wet, and stinking of turps. His mother stood anxiously in the kitchen. He could see from his mother's face something was wrong. Dick saw his dad sat at the table so he knew it was not his father. His mother was holding something in her red calloused hands. She gave the pale cream envelope to her oldest child. He slowly opened the letter. He gulped when he read that he was to attend a medical on May 16th. William turned round holding his conscription letter. Dick looked confused, his father was forty seven years of age. Britain was so desperate for men they moved the age to fifty one.

Charlotte looked at her eldest child's fresh, young, handsome face. Her heart sank, she hoped the war would have been over and that Dick might be saved from being conscripted into the army. Her thoughts went to Roath train station. The station was being used as a reception centre for wounded soldiers. Later, soldiers were moved to Splottlands Board School, The school was now a hospital. Charlotte saw some of the soldiers and noticed their injuries and her heart froze. She thought, *Would this damn war change him, or kill him? Her mind screamed. Take William instead, take the man who broke my heart, take him and leave my son home!*

Richard Charles Griffin passed his medical and was

conscripted into The South Wales Borderers. He travelled to Aldershot and Monmouth barracks for six months'training. Months later, Dick gingerly walked up Railway Street in full uniform. He could see his mother and two sisters waiting on the doorstep.

His two brothers, Victor and James, were waiting at the top of the street. Victor shouted, "Here he is."

"All right, Vic, keep it quiet," Dick meekly replied.

Dick felt irritated by his uniform, it made his skin itch and the boots drew too much attention. The tin, tin noise of metal hitting tar made him feel more uncomfortable. He thought, *Far too late, half the street is out.* His father came out and shook his son's hand. Dick was taken aback by this public show of affection. His mother wiped a tear and sighed. "Richard, you do not look old enough to be in the army." His father remained home, he failed his medical. Acute bronchitis left him with a weak heart.

Dick and his family stood at Cardiff General train station along with other families. Charlotte's heart was heavy and she sighed deeply. She looked to her son, who weighed eight stone, and was 5 feet 6 inches tall. She knew Dick had no choice, he was conscripted in, and you did not ask why, you did as you were told. She prayed and hoped he survived.

Dick saw his mate, Harry, and his family coming towards him, both nodded to each other shyly. The train guard blew his whistle to let the train driver know it was time to go. The train let out steam, coal and soot into the autumn air. Shouts of, "Do not forget to write, we will send you parcels of food and baccy," echoed. Then the sound of the train doors slamming shut. Dick waved until the curve in the train track took his family out of view. He and Harry shared a carriage with other new recruits. Dick felt emotional, so he rolled a cigarette and kept his emotions in check.

On a damp October morning they set sail from Dover to Calais. Despite it being late autumn, the channel was calm, like a mill pond, the leaded grey mirrored the deep grey sky. The colours matched Dick's mood. He decided to stay on the deck and look back at what he was leaving behind.

At Calais, Dick and Harry were greeted by a sea of soldiers from all parts of the Empire. Some were going home, others were arriving.

The following day, the sun threaded a gold light as Dick stretched his cold, aching body. He quickly ate his small amount of vittles, rolled a cigarette, breathed in the weed and looked around at the mass of khaki. Two by two they marched to the train station for their journey to Ledeghem, Ypres.

They arrived at 9 pm and were put in a large barn with others. The two rookies walked in on a right hue and cry. An officer was demanding that soldiers showed their pay book before any blankets could be issued. The backlash and the rising tempers of the tired and hungry troops soon put paid to this affair. Blankets were issued, but no food. Dick was starving, Harry had some home made cake leftover, he shared this with his childhood friend, they managed to find some weak tea to help wash the cake down. "This tea is terrible," Dick said to Harry, "it is like dish water." Both friends found some space, and prepared to get some shut eye. Dick's belly sang a hungry tune and it was not a lullaby.

Dick and his new comrades had never seen so much mud and water. As Dick marched he thought of home and the reason why he was in this sodden, soaked country. They marched through St Omer, Hasbrouck, where some of the sights unnerved some of the young soldiers. The stench of death and despair that war brought hung on to their moral fibre. Just before they arrived at Ypres, a parcel arrived from home. Biscuits, baccy, woollen socks, letters from his sisters and one from his mother.

131

While shaving, Dick saw three British scouting aeroplanes come up from the rear and meet with another plane coming from the line. The sound of machine gun fire rattled his insides. Dick shouted, "Harry." Both looked up to the skies and a dog fight.

Harry said, "The single plane is trying to get away."

"He won't get far, that scout will have him."

The scout tracked the plane back to earth. Bullets pinged all around and Harry and Dick both dived under the wagon. Later, Corporal Henry Duggan informed them that the plane was British and was camouflaged. Jerry often took our planes for their own. The scouts had a bad feeling and went by their gut and drowned the plane. There had been several incidents lately of Germans flying our machines that they had captured at some point or another. One of the airman was slightly wounded, the other was unhurt.

Night time came and Dick was on guard duty. A full moon, with a blanket of stars, kept him company. Suddenly silence was broken by the bombing from British aeroplanes. Dick thought some were flying so low that you could spit on them. As dawn rose, Dick was about to retire, suddenly there was shelling and chaos. One man was killed instantly. Then the ex Salvation Army man, whom Dick liked, was blown to pieces. "Talk about Onward, Christian Soldiers, he ain't walking anywhere," one Tommy chipped in.

Humour can easily arise from fear. The noise, hunger, the smell of burnt flesh, and rats, mixed in with mud added fear, sometimes terror in others, it was enough to send any sane person over the edge, and it did. Mental exhaustion had no class or background. It affected solicitors, bankers, and farm labourers and these were the men that made up the Battalion.

Dick finished writing letters back home and began to sew parts of his uniform. He felt the autumn rays on his light skinned face, then he closed his eyes and dreamed of swimming in the open air lido at Splott Park with Harry and others. The screech of war brought him back to reality and reminded him of where he really was. Hell!

News came through that Jerry had evacuated Kemmel Hill. The British had held throughout July and August. Rumours were going around the Battalion that there was talk of peace and that there might be a truce. They marched through towns and villages and saw the different Allied flags that were on display. They noticed a lot of chalk marks on doors and Dick thought, *This war must be coming to an end.*

They marched sixteen miles that day. Rations were

133

found from somewhere, the boys were too tired to ask or care. They eat their vittles and bedded down on a straw mattress, soon sound asleep. They were woken by a rattling noise. Dick rubbed his eyes, and noticed a soldier riding a bicycle that had no tyres, rubber being scarce. It was a German bike, and who ever owned the bike had bound helical springs, around the wheels. They were bound together by an exterior band of iron, and it made an awful racket.

For the next couple of days, they remained on the German and Belgium border. When word got out that there might be an armistice, Dick nudged Harry in the ribs, both smiled at each other. This did not mean they could let their guard down, they were still at war!

Dick and others were ordered to look out for emissaries coming over with white flags, and to keep their eyes and wits intact just in case they were attacked. They walked over makeshift pontoons, the river was high and flowing from all the rain and the men were deafened to other sounds. They could not hear the Germans taking pot shots. This was Dick and Harry's first taste of sniper war. Suddenly, Harry slipped, Dick grabbed his friend, there was no response. Dick saw the blood from a head wound and saw Harry's eye was halfway down his cheek. He felt sick and began to tremble, yet he held onto his childhood friend. An officer shouted, "Get Griffin away now!" Other soldiers picked Harry up. All were safely across, except Harry. The first time in his young life Dick broke down and cried.

They walked into a bigger town where a Catholic procession was taking place, fronted by a small boy with a lantern and ringing some bells. As the procession approached, the crowd of bystanders, men and woman, fell to their knees into the mud, muttering blessings. This startled Dick, he thought they were mad, he thought the whole world was mad!

On November 11th, 1918, they were told at 9.08am, hostilities would cease. Dick could not believe what he was hearing, he looked around him. Smiles were stretched on men's faces but not Dick's, Dick thought war was cruel and evil. He could not express his opinion, but he knew the poet soldiers would write the truth in verse. The German army was beaten, and on November 11th, 1918, they dutifully signed to that effect.

Dick went home on leave and late one night, after the family went to bed, Dick, in the silence, broke down to his mother and told her of the horrors of war and the death of his childhood friend, Harry. She held her eldest child and cradled him as if he was a baby.

Part of the Armistice agreement allowed advancement on to German soil. Four armies, each one from the principal allied powers that fought on the Western Front: The British, including Empire troops, French, Americans and Belgians. The joint decision was not to march on Berlin but, instead, seize one of Germany's economic and commercial jewels, "The Rhineland." Once across the Rhine, the Allies waited while the provisions of the peace treaty, were being hammered out at Versailles. Britain took control of Cologne, and remained there for six years.
British troops lived among a generally friendly and largely law-abiding population. Dick stayed for one year…..

Ireland's War for Independence / Anglo Irish War

1919 -1921

Britain embarked on its infamous divide and rule strategy.
Lloyd George knew this would divide Irish against Irish,
thereby leading Michael Collins into signing his own death
warrant. Ireland was falling apart. The six Counties had now
gone and their allegiance to the crown was still in place. But
Ireland had a chance to make inroads to a permanent
independence and instead chose bloody civil war. It chose
war because a Republic of Ireland could be achieved.
Ireland wanted to break free from Britain, Britain refused, so
war ensued. Britain was at WAR WITH ITS OWN!! From the
streets of Dublin, the west coast of Ireland, to the top of
Donegal.

December 1919. The 1st Battalion of the South Wales
Borderers left Cologne and travelled to Ireland, they were
stationed at Dunshauglin. Dunshauglin was 18 miles from
Dublin. The British army was trained in a different way, and
how they were trained was of little use in Ireland. Their
combat experience was futile too. The military force
deployed in Ireland was there to keep law and order, a 'Peace
Keeping Force,' they were inadequate for the task in numbers
and training. Ireland was still under British rule. The Welsh
Borderers were fighting their own people and this was
painful.

This war had no trench war, it was urban, your enemy you did not recognise. The enemy were ordinary men, women and children. The IRA used tactics from the Boer War. They dressed like everyone else, this was Guerrilla Warfare. The experience of the Boer war, from the British perspective, had long been forgotten.

The British fought a campaign whose objectives were unclear from the beginning, and where policy was split between Dublin and London. There was no conflict of intelligence in Ireland. MI5 had their hands full back home in Britain. They were dealing with the threat of Bolshevism, due to the rise of the Russian Revolution and Bolshevism, replacing Tsar Nicolas.

The Anglo Irish War / War of Independence could not be won by the British soldier alone. The RIC, were under a separate command and control. They brought international opprobrium due to their use of torture, and in turn alienated themselves from the public. 'The Black and Tans,' and the 'Auxiliary Division,' were brought in to fill in where the average British soldier could not achieve. SHEER TERROR!!

This, in turn, created more martyrs, and some say the propaganda machine for Sinn Féin to use and pump out. Britain did not do itself any favours, its reputation in Ireland, over seven hundred years, was not good. The taking of land and the Gaelic language, which was the back bone of Irish identity. The famine, the dilatory approval to the introduction of 'Home Rule,' The Easter Rising of 1916, was the abscess that needed to be lanced and the killing of the sixteen men, after 1916 was the open wound. The anger and the injustice flowed out of this festering sore, and it was volcanic.

Dick liked the Irish, he was surrounded by them back home, he went to school with them, his next door neighbours were Irish. Where he lived was known as Little Ireland. He had grown up with stories about Ireland and the Famine. His granddad was Irish.

Dick was on patrol in Dublin, he avoided looking at the buildings, historic or commercial. He looked at the masses of people that passed by, some appeared friendly, some were indifferent, others showed hate. Dick soon realised that Dublin was not Cologne. There was no welcome. He felt the intense hatred and was confused, the Irish that he knew back home were not like this. The soldiers were ordered to get out of the wagon and march in twos.

Dick felt something wet on his face, a woman passing by had spat at him. The woman, who was dressed so elegantly, every inch a lady, ran into the crowd. "Bitch," he

140

said out loud, as he wiped the spit with his uniform sleeve. "God, you can't go by appearance," said Dick to his comrade in arms, Dai. David Llewellyn was a Corporal and was two years older than Dick, he came from Abergavenny. A stocky man, with dark hair and good looks, good looks counted for nothing in Ireland.

They approached a couple of suspicious looking young men, not much older than they were. "Stop, do not go any further, and put your hands above your head!!"

The two men looked at the British soldiers with contempt, yet still obeyed the order. One of the men leaned forward and whispered in Dick's ear, "A fecker, you were not invited in, so when are you going to get out of my country."

"What did you just say?"

"Ah, to be sure, I have not said a thing."

This was Dick's first patrol in Dublin and he had been spat at and told, more than once, to feck off home. "At least you knew your enemy in France and Germany. They wore a different uniform, here it could be anyone," Dick informed his senior colleague.

In the late nineteenth century, the British Army was very much part of everyday Irish life and many Irishmen joined the British Army. Relationships with local women were quite common. However, with the radicalisation of Irish nationalism from the early twentieth century onwards, fraternisation was much frowned upon and the radical nationalist, Maude Gonne MacBride, was leading groups of activists who apprehended women keeping company with soldiers on the streets of Dublin...

The nature of the situation that Dick was under created paranoia, they were in someone else's country. The enemy knew the terrain, alley, sewer lid, the docks and the countryside. All Dick was trained for was the trenches and dug outs. Ireland affected his mind, he had never experienced hate like this. It seeped out from every quarter. Dick patrolled the area with Robbie Brown. Robbie was always joking and always saw the brighter side to life and Dick liked him for it. Dick's regiment had moved to Richmond Barracks. The Black and Tans and the Auxiliary Division, moved to Dunshauglin.

Dick and Robbie were on night guard duty outside Richmond Barracks when they befriended some of the old Irish. They often shared a cigarette with some. One was a tramp, he was a great story teller. He would tell the two friends about the abuse and the squalor that the Irish had to live under and 'The Great Lockout' of 1913. Dick would relay the stories he heard back home in Cardiff. The late night conversations that took place began to soften Dick's and Robbie's heart. "After all, we are all Celts," said Dick with a smile.

Dick and Robbie had been in Dublin six months when they were on guard duty outside Leinster Sewing Factory. Over time through banter, they got to know some of the girls that worked at the factory. Some of the women would openly flirt with the two young soldiers. There was one that never took part. She was short, petite, with long chestnut brown hair. This woman fascinated Dick and he would often stare at her. He sometimes saw her in 'Carolans' pub singing along to the many songs and ballads but she never went near the soldiers.

One morning the young petite woman had had enough, she turned to her friend Ruth, "I know he is looking at me, the cheek of it."

Ruth was short, with a shock of red hair that never looked tidy. She said tartly to her feisty friend, "He is, Mag, and is looking at you again!"

"How dare he, I am not putting up with this." The woman made her way to where the two soldiers were. The taller one of the two said, "Stop, madam, you cannot come any closer," as he aimed his rifle at her.

Through gritted teeth, she replied, "You tell him to stop staring at me."

"Madam, it is a free country, he can look where he likes," said the older soldier.

"Free country, my country is not free, as long as you are here!" The two girls ran away, half in fear and half in fun.

Dick felt odd, a strange sensation poured through him, surging through his veins. He felt light headed and he felt as if he knew the woman in another life. He told himself, *Get a grip man, she is the enemy and you are in her country.* Maggie sat at her sewing machine and her mind drifted back to the British soldier. He was not cocky like some of the soldiers. She chastised herself, *God behave, he's a Brit!*

One autumn morning she was late, there was a fine drizzle, she was flustered, her boots clip clopped on the cobble stones, when suddenly she slipped and fell. Dick saw her and helped her to her feet, she glared at him and said, "Get away from me." This did not deter him, he was smitten.

A week later Maggie went to work early, she was making a skirt, Maggie made all her own clothes. She carried a large bag with her skirt inside. She clip clopped past the soldiers, nose in the air. Suddenly she fell again, her bag went one way, she the other. Dick picked up her bag and gingerly approached her. Maggie stopped, her deep blue eyes fell into his turquoise blue eyes, and, for the first time in her life, Maggie blushed. Dick gave her the bag and inside he left a note. She brushed herself down, sat at her machine, took the skirt out and a note fell on her lap. She quickly hid the note. Later, in the ladies toilet, she opened the note with shaking hands.

I do not mean to stare at you but I find you truly beautiful. This poem was written by Rupert Brooke, I copied this verse for you:

> *"Someday I will rise and leave my friends*
> *and seek you again through the world's far end*
> *you whom I found so fair"*

Richard.

Maggie was speechless, no one had ever written to her before, let alone a poem. She felt strange, as if she had been taken over by somebody else. The following morning he waited for her. Maggie tried to steady and compose herself. She felt the redness creep from her neck and spread across her cheeks. As she drew near, her heart rate quickened, then Dick discreetly gave her another note.

Maggie sat at her machine and stared ahead, she had never known feelings like this before, she had only known poverty, grief, anger and violence, and, along with most of Dublin, she was still traumatised by 1916. She had only known fear! Now she felt butterflies in her belly, a rush of warmness, adrenalin poured like liquid gold through her veins. This clouded her judgment of the danger. Her mind warned her, but her heart told her to ignore the warnings.

She glanced at the note and nearly dropped it, when the supervisor noticed Maggie had stopped sewing and said, "Margaret, you cannot sew men's shirts while daydreaming." Maggie slipped the note into her pocket and later, in the ladies, she opened it. She gasped and mumbled, "Oh, he has lovely handwriting."

Dear Maggie,
I know your name because I hear your friends call you Maggie.My name is Richard but known as Dick. Though I see your beautiful face during the week. I would very much like to take a stroll with you, to hold your hand in mine and to hear you talk.
Dick.

Maggie felt dizzy, the butterflies rising in her belly

brought her back. She held her breath, then deep breathed and reread the note. Later that night, lying in bed next to Chrissie, her mother in the other small bed snored, she thought on the soldier and his love note. Plans to meet with Dick flew around her head.

At breakfast the following morning, Maggie's eyes were full of sleep. Her mother turned from the porridge pan and gently spoke, "Maggie, are you all right, you look a bit peaky."

Chrissie interrupted her mother, "Maggie, you tossed and turned all night, disturbing my sleep."

Maggie looked up confused and then she sharply replied, "Oh, I am sorry, I think it is that time of the month, and, Chrissie, after your marriage next week, the bed will be all mine!"

Outside the factory, Maggie slyly handed Dick a note with instructions inside to meet the following Sunday, at Phoenix Park. Maggie knew the park well, all the nooks and crannies and the hideaways. She instructed Dick to make his way to the lake and opposite the lake, there's a small woodland, meet me by the second oak tree...

It was a bright morning, Saturday morning. The boys were

outside in the yard grooming the horses, washing down the carts, streams of white satin ribbon hung on the line ready to be made into bows and then attached to the cart. Inside the kitchen, laughter filled the air. Maggie was helping Chrissie into her wedding dress that she helped to make. She was doing up the last pearl button on the high neck dress with the lace bodice, length just above the ankle. On her feet she wore off-white kitten heeled shoes and then the veil and headdress with its pale, lilac coloured, tiny satin roses. "Chrissie, you look beautiful," gasped Maggie.

Mary wiped a tear and gave Chrissie a bouquet of long stemmed lavender and small headed gypsophila tied in a lavender ribbon. Maggie wore a suit she had made, and on her head the latest fashionable hat called a cloche, the French word meant bell. The hat was grey with a lavender band which matched her light grey suit and pale lilac blouse. Mary wore a black chiffon, long dress. The boys were in black suits. Alec was to give Chrissie away and he was very nervous. He elbowed Christy and said, "Good job you are taking the cart."

The family drove the small way to the church at Arran Quay. Along the way some waved, others cheered. Inside the church, family and friends filled the pews. At the altar stood Michael, but not in his IRA uniform, he wore a dark suit with a lilac waistcoat and green tie. Michael's best man was his brother, Liam, both stood ramrod straight. Chrissie walked down the aisle, holding the arm of her nineteen-year-old brother Alec, behind came Maggie and her mother with Christy and James following.

Afterwards, they celebrated with drinks and food and a beautiful three-tier cake that Mary made. Lots of laughter and singing, and the singing of rebel songs that made Maggie go cold, creating goosebumps on her arms.

For their honeymoon the newly weds were travelling to Bray and were to stay at a hotel for one night. Chrissie wore a beige suit, a fake fox stole and a wide brimmed hat. Alec piped up and said, "Chrissie, you look just like a film star, what's her name? I know, Greta Garbo." Chrissie smiled and so did Michael. Chrissie threw her bouquet and Maggie caught it with one outstretched hand.

Sunday came, it was a lovely, colourful, autumnal morning. Maggie did not want to wear the suit and fashionable hat she wore to the wedding, she did not want to draw attention. She put on her cream blouse with lace on the collar and cuffs and a cream skirt. Because Maggie made all her own clothes, they fitted her small frame perfectly. She polished her brown leather shoes with the four inch heel. She needed the height, being only four feet and ten inches tall. Her long chestnut brown hair she put up in a bun, with a gold clasp. This kept her hair neatly in place. No makeup, only a dab of lavender on her wrists. Her white lace handkerchief she placed in her brown bag, along with some money. All the while her heart fluttered and a smile appeared when she thought of Richard. Especially his eyes and the way he looked at her.

It was warm for September, she decided not to wear her coat and chose a jacket. She kissed her mother goodbye. Maggie's passionate feelings for the soldier turned her into a liar! For the first time in her young life, she lied to her mother when she told her she was going for a stroll with Ruth to the park.

The tram stopped at the park gates, she alighted the tram, looked up, not a cloud in the sky, bronze and burnt orange tinged the leaves on the trees. As she walked up the winding path, the sun warmed her back and birdsong filled the air. Her heart was beating so fast, she hummed a tune to herself. Walking towards her were a handsome couple. The woman was tall and looked elegant, the man was taller and his hair was raven black. As the handsome couple drew near Maggie recognised the woman. It was Lily Murphy. Lily and her family were poor, they lived in one room with her mam and dad and seven siblings. Maggie stopped, then spoke, "Is that you, Lily Murphy?"

The tall woman stopped and looked down on Maggie, put her gloved hand to her mouth, and gasped, "Good God, Maggie Caffery. I cannot believe it is you." The two childhood friends chatted. Maggie noticed how beautiful Lily looked. She remembered when Lily's hair was lank and how she never looked clean. Maggie often took her back to where she lived. Lily would come over all shy, she felt conscious of not being clean like Maggie. She was aware of how grubby her dress looked and where her mam got the dress from. She often wore handouts from the St Vincent de Paul Society.

Maggie remembered the first time Lily came to her home. "Come in, Lily, we won't bite, it is only me sister, Essie, and me little brothers, you will be fine." The family often shared food with Lily. Lily never ever forgot the kindness Maggie had showed her. Unbeknown to Maggie, Lily was engaged to a senior member of the IRA, Dermot O'Hara. Ten years previous, Lily's family was the talk of Dublin. The family suddenly disappeared because they owed money and, instead of paying up they moved to England.

Lily's skin looked radiant, her strawberry blonde hair looked lovely in a bun. Maggie could see, beneath her soft light brown coat, that Lily's dress was pale yellow. She held herself like a real lady. Dermot looked around while the long lost friends chatted. Dermot could never switch off, always on the job. He also wondered why Maggie was walking alone. Dermot coughed and inquired why Maggie was walking alone. Maggie let out a nervous laugh and replied, "I am meeting my friend Ruth." Maggie and Lily exchanged addresses, and said their goodbyes.

Lily and her family moved to England, where Lily excelled in school, and later went on to become a school teacher. However, she knew one day she would return. Lily met Dermot in London; he worked for the GPO. A lot of Irish youngsters left Ireland for a better life in Britain and would often send money back home. The Irish in London formed their own clique, and they had their own community and social circle.

After a while Dermot told Lily about the IRB, the Irish Republican Brotherhood. Lily was enthralled, and she never forgot her roots and the poverty she endured. Lily found a teaching post in Ireland and returned. The lovers often wrote to each other. Lily joined the women's wing of the IRB. Dermot was called back after the 1916 'Easter Rising' and the bloody executions, when the other remaining rebels were sent to Frongoch, North Wales.

Maggie looked back at the handsome couple and, as she did, Dermot turned round and stared hard at her. Suddenly pangs of guilt pierced her mind. She thought, *he knows I am up to no good*. Maggie felt nervous, her knees knocked and her belly tumbled.

Dick was wearing his civilian clothes and was hiding behind the second oak tree. His eyes were on Maggie, and, as she drew near, he could see her clear complexion, no makeup and her eyes deep blue. She then smiled. Dick had never seen a smile like it, her smile radiated beauty, lit up her face and melted Dick's heart.

Dick greeted Maggie, Maggie whispered, "What am I like meeting with an English soldier?"

"Me English, I am Welsh, with a bit of Irish thrown in from the potato famine on me grandfather's side."

Maggie backed away. Dick reached out and held Maggie's hand and kissed it. Maggie noticed his eyes again, turquoise in colour, this sent an electric force that soared through her veins. This warmed her heart and made her eyes shine and her cheeks glowed. She was on the edge, and staring in to something that was forbidden, she turned quickly and fled the park.

Monday, September 20th, 1920. It was a clear autumn day and a young medical student was making his way to 8 o'clock mass. He strode out, a fit healthy man, wearing a tweed suite, looking no different to any other Irish student. The oak door creaked as he entered the church, the smell of incense burning candles and wood wormed wood comforted him. The pews were full of women. The church was the only place of refuge for them, and the only place where they found peace and quiet.

The young dark haired man was also a Section Commander in the IRA. He joined the queue to the altar. He knelt down and his innocent face lifted up open-mouthed to receive the body of Christ. The wafer thin bread stuck to the roof of his mouth, the wine helped to flush it away. He walked back to the bare wooded pew, knelt and prayed. He looked to his watch, it was eight thirty. "Ete Missa est," the priest said.

"Deo Gratias," the congregation responded. They all stood up, waited for the priest to pass and they followed like sheep.

Outside, the flock was greeted by the crisp earthy smell of autumn. Kevin Barry shook the priest's hand and thanked him for the mass, then bade him farewell. The young rebel then made his way towards O'Connell Street and

Mountjoy Square. He had a meeting with his friend and fellow student, Frank Flood. He checked his inside pocket, everything was where it should be.

His mind wandered to the medical exam that was taking place that afternoon at 2pm. He saw his friend, they made small talk. They were aware that Dublin was full of spies, and they trusted no one. The two young men left Mountjoy Square and headed for Bolton Street and the bakers. They went their separate ways along Bolton Street and window shopped. Kevin Barry glanced to his watch, the vehicle was late, he looked around him, saw Edmond Foley and Patrick Maher, they tilted their hats in unison.

The young Section Commander looked at his reflection in the window. He heard the truck before he saw it. His heart raced, his mouth was dry, just the stale taste of the wine from the morning's communion. He trusted his men to do what they had been trained to do. He noticed a tramp sat in the gutter, spluttering and coughing. The British army truck pulled up, a soldier got out. Kevin Barry pulled out his semi-automatic black pistol, that fitted his hand like a glove and shouted, "Stop there!"

Four British soldiers were at the back of the vehicle with their Mauser rifles at the ready. The British soldiers climbed out of the truck. Then, a shot pierced the air, and all hell broke loose. Hand to hand conflict took place. Kevin Barry's semi-automatic locked not once, but twice. The rebels panicked, they ran from the conflict. Kevin Barry hid under the vehicle that he hoped to capture. It was now his safe haven. He tried to control his breathing, his palms sweated while above him was chaos. His mind went blank, empty of any thoughts. He lay there, the stink of the petrol fumes made him want to cough, but he held his breath. The gravel from the road dug into his back as if he were lying on a bed of nails.

An old tramp was sitting in the gutter, he looked sideways and locked eyes on the young medical student whose eyes were full of fear. "Don't worry, yer secret is safe with me," said the tramp, as he tapped his nose and winked at Kevin Barry.

Unbeknown to the tramp a British officer witnessed all. "Quick men, there is one under the vehicle." Kevin felt hands on his boots, he was dragged from his hiding place, his head bounced on the gravel and two soldiers pulled him to his feet. His mind raced, his heart pounded, and his bowels wanted relieving. He was aware of the sea of Irish people but he was alone, he had no one to protect him. He thought, *Is this what Christ felt like in the Garden of Gethsemane?*

He felt the wood of the rifle sting his mouth. He ran

his tongue along his teeth. The blood in his mouth tasted metallic but no teeth were missing. He saw a young woman quickly turn away. It was Maggie's turn to buy the cakes from the local bakers. Maggie had been warned by her supervisor to be careful of snipers, the Auxiliaries and 'Black and Tans.' Maggie liked taking risks. She noticed the commotion, everyone stopped what they were doing, and became spectators to Kevin Barry's arrest.

Maggie saw the soldiers, and the handsome young rebel who was being dragged from underneath the car. She then witnessed, and heard the smack of the soldier's rifle and saw the blood spurt from the young rebel's face. Maggie looked away, she felt sick. As she turned away, she saw two, painfully thin, young British soldiers before her, one was Dick. A ball of bile rose from her churning belly and she spat the bile into her hankie.

The young martyr was thrown into the back of the truck. Three soldiers then kicked and punched the young rebel senseless. Kevin Barry was numb, numb with shock, he went beyond pain, and he sat up motionless. The British soldiers then laid their dead comrade, Private Harold Washington, in the back of the army truck, below Kevin Barry's feet. Barry stared into space and avoided what lay in front of him. A young soldier whispered. "A gift from us, you Irish bastard," and punched him again.

Back in the sewing factory, Maggie shook and thought, *God what am I doing?* The smell of cordite mixed with blood, but most of all the smell of fear, that had emanated from Kevin Barry made her feel nausea.

Two Welsh soldiers arrived at the scene, their hearts were pumping. They were nervous because at Ypres their enemy wore a different uniform. In Ireland, their enemy looked like normal people going about their business. The young Welsh soldier turned to his colleague and said, "The one they had captured looks so young, a boy not much older than me."

The soldiers dispersed the crowd and replaced the shocking violent scene with law and order. People turned away to get on with day to day things, but in their hearts and minds was Kevin Barry.

After work, in the cold autumn night, Maggie and her family made the pilgrimage, along with many others, to Mountjoy Prison to stand in a vigil and to pray and hope the power of prayer would save Kevin Barry from being executed. Their hopes and prayers were in vain. Michael quietly told Maggie and Chrissie, "Kevin Barry at the time was the only one captured. Michael Collins tried his best to get the young rebel out of British hands but to no avail. The Castle was filled to the brim with British soldiers." Both sisters wiped their eyes. Kevin Barry was brutally tortured, but he would not say, tell, or speak of what he knew. Barry was loyal to the cause till the very end. Kevin Barry saw himself as an Irish soldier, fighting for a free Ireland. He looked upon the British soldier as withholding that freedom. Kevin Barry was condemned in a military court, he asked to be shot by a firing squad but his request was refused. He was hung by the British on November 1st, 1920.

"Kevin Barry gave his young life for the cause of Liberty."

By executing someone as young as Kevin Barry, the British handed the IRA a huge propaganda victory! Young men flocked to join the IRA and to fight in Ireland's War of Independence. Kevin Barry, Patrick Moran, Frank Flood, Thomas Whelan, Thomas Traynor, Patrick Doyle, Thomas Bryan, Bernard Ryan, Edmond Foley, and Patrick Maher were all hanged for taking part in Ireland's War of Independence. They were known as The Forgotten Ten.

The IRA campaign was more widespread. It was directed at civilians, who could be regarded as giving comfort to the enemy as well as the police, and soldiers, and was accompanied by attacks on public buildings. The British responded by sending ex-soldiers into Ireland called the 'Black and Tans' due to their uniforms, being khaki green, with black belts, and a peaked cap of the RIC. They were ruled by Auxiliaries, ex-army officers, who acted as an ill-disciplined, semi-military force. The 'Black and Tans' were barbaric; their officers told them to shoot to kill, no questions asked, bloody murderers!

After Kevin Barry's demise, Maggie did not see Dick for weeks, he was on patrol duties elsewhere in Dublin. She felt she had betrayed herself, but as the days passed the betrayal she felt had passed.

On a cold Monday, Maggie walked towards her place of work when she saw Dick, her heart lurched forward and her belly was full of butterflies. She took a deep breath and walked past the soldiers as if she never had a secret liaison. Dick stood near and spoke, "Excuse me, miss, you dropped your hankie." She stared wide-eyed and blushed, he smiled and gave her the hankie with a note inside. She discreetly put it inside her pocket. They side glanced one another. Maggie felt as if a magnetic force was pulling her towards the British soldier. Maggie and Dick never met in Phoenix Park again.

They both knew it was dangerous and, if caught, they would pay and pay dearly.

The lovers were in love, insanely in love and this strong emotion crushed their fear. They would see each other at the pub for brief moments, he would hold her hand as she walked past. They left love notes for each other behind a loose stone in the wall near her home. After some time Dick stopped calling in at the pub, it was far too dangerous. Often they would meet and have small encounters, sit and just stare into each other's eyes in a longing silence. They were young and in love and their love had replaced any logic or any sense of danger. Dick would forget he was a British soldier and what he was doing was wrong.

However, Maggie sometimes felt she was drowning in guilt, her mind in turmoil. Ireland was fighting for independence, and the very thing that she and her family had always wanted. She was torn in two, yet desire for the soldier always won.

One night she whispered to Dick, "I sometimes feel I cannot go on living this lie."

Dick replied, "My time in the army is coming to an end. We can make a life together."
Maggie smiled, "You can leave Wales and live here in Dublin."

"Maggie, I want to be where you are and I am willing to leave everything behind for you." Behind the back lane the secret lovers embraced and passionately kissed.

Mary noticed a change in Maggie. She had lost weight and her personality was no longer bubbly. One morning at breakfast Mary said, "Maggie, who you mooning over?" There was no reply. Maggie was not there, in her heart she was with the British soldier but the fear of betrayal was knocking on the wall of her conscience. Mary slammed her hand down on the table. Maggie jumped and spilt her cup of tea. "Now look at the mess you made." Maggie quickly cleared up. Mary tartly spoke again "Who you mooning over?"

Maggie's face reddened and tears pricked her eyes. "I am not mooning over anyone, Mammy." Mary gave her daughter a look that made Maggie's legs shake. She grabbed her coat and flew out the door.

On the morning of November 21st, 1920, in Dublin, eleven English civilians, believed to be working for British intelligence, would be shot dead by the IRA in their homes and at hotels. In the afternoon the 'Black and Tans' wreaked revenge.

"How yer doing, Frankie?" said Alec as he paid his friend the money for his and Christy's tickets.

"Could be better, Alec, but you just got to carry on."

"Aye, to be sure, keep the faith, Frankie." Frankie was a friend of Alec's, he was a well known ticket seller but he had fallen on hard times. His wife died leaving him to bring up four children on his own. "See you soon, Frankie."

The two brothers walked through the turnstile and made their way to the stand and their seats, they were at the centre and four rows back from the front behind the goal post. "It is a grand view, we have here, Alec," Christy said, while rubbing his hands together and then blowing on them. "Ah, I think winter is coming early."

"To be sure," his brother replied.
The crowd was huge. 'Croke Park' was full to the brim with men, women and children. Dublin was playing Tipperary and kick off was at 2.45pm. "Hey, Alec what's the delay, they should have kicked off 10 minutes ago."

"Yes, it's strange."

The boys could just about hear each other with all the noise from the boisterous happy crowd. It would be another twenty minutes before the game commenced. At 3.15pm the referee blew his whistle, and a huge roar went up from both sets of fans.

It was a fierce game, very competitive, both boys cheered on their teams. Alec saw Frankie McGuire, the ticket seller, run into the stadium. Alec thought, *That's unusual ,he seems to be shouting something.* Outside and unseen by the crowd, British security forces were advancing towards the Park. The police, Auxiliaries and 'Black and Tans' approached the Park from the south and canal end. They were ordered to surround the grounds, guard the exits and search every man in the Park. Frankie noticed the military armoured car. Frankie knew you never exposed yourself needlessly when a military vehicle was about.

The ticket sellers were the ears and eyes for Michael Collins, they all belonged to the IRA. Frankie mumbled, "Feck, the fecking bastards, shit." Frankie, a short, thin man, threw his fag butt away and ran into the stadium to alarm the others and also to protect himself, his children needing him. He was even contemplating leaving Ireland for America. He knew his children deserved a better future. He knew in his heart things would get worse for Ireland before there would be any peace.

Alec grabbed Christy when he heard the first shot. The spectators were startled when a volley of shots were fired from inside of the turnstile entrance. Alec noticed armed and uniformed men entering the field, his mind was alarmed and fear rose in him, he looked at Christy, who was as white as a sheet. Alec knew there was nowhere to run or hide, they were sitting targets. The air stank of cordite, blood and urine. "Jesus, Mary and Joseph," cried the man next to him, whose girl friend was slumped over his body, blood flowed, flowed on to their shoes and boots. Christy felt sick, he began to retch, nothing came up.

The noise from the enemy weapons was deafening, the sound of human beings screaming created sheer terror. Alec took off his scarf and tried to tie it around some of the woman's wounds. To no avail, she was dead. Her poor fiancé just rocked back and fore, holding on to his beloved, who had already gone to another place.

At first people were shocked then confused, this was soon replaced by fear and panic, and the fear and panic spread as quickly as the bullets that were being fired. The spectators made a rush for the far side of Croke Park. The British continued to fire shots over their heads, and into the crowd. The two brothers stayed close. Christy looked towards the pitch, he noticed a Tipperary player had been shot and witnessed a young fan kneeling by the player's side as if in prayer. Then the fan fell over, he had been shot by a coward wearing a British uniform.

Christy screamed, "GOD, ALEC, THIS IS HELL WE

ARE IN HELL!"

Alec, still in shock, looked to his little brother and choked, "Christy, we will be all right, trust me." Alec felt terror in his throat, but he never showed his true feelings to his younger brother. The scene of bloody madness subsided after ninety seconds. A happy family sporting event turned into a nightmare of violence and death.

When Mary heard about the violent, cowardly act, she fell to her knees. She knew her two healthy young sons had gone to the game, "MOTHER OF GOD, NO, NO!" she screamed.

The two sisters, Chrissie and Maggie, were out on a stroll when they heard the news. Chrissie fled, running to nowhere. She knew her brothers had gone to the game, she also knew that Michael was on some assignment and she had not heard from him for a week. "Chrissie, Chrissie, wait for me," Maggie shouted breathlessly, her heart pounding in her chest, and beads of sweat laced her brow.

Chrissie stopped running and through tears, she spoke to her sister. "Maggie, how long can this violence continue? I cannot bare it any longer. I wish Michael and I emigrated to America!" Maggie leaned against her sister, her hand on her shoulder. Both sisters looked at each other and said, "Mammy, my God, Mammy!"

They both prayed all the way back to Red Cow Lane. Breathlessly, they barged into the kitchen. Mary was sat at the table, her head in her hands. James sat rocking back and forth, he knew his mammy was upset, but he was helpless in his vulnerability. The two women put their arms around their mother. Mary let the tears flow, and sobbed loudly, this scared Maggie, she had never seen her Mammy cry like this before. Maggie was hurt, hurt for her mammy, Chrissie and her younger brothers. She was now scared for herself and she had every reason to be. The bloodshed and the cold blooded murder did not rest in Maggie's belly, she felt sick, sick with fear of being caught. Yet, the thought of not seeing Dick again stabbed at her heart and pained her mind. She cried for her and Dick, and their very uncertain future.

The three women sobbed together. James sat, hopeless in his innocence, witnessing the women he loved fall apart. Chrissie got up and put the kettle on the stove with a heavy heart. Maggie and her mother stared into space. The lamp lighter came round to light the lamps creating an orange glow along the yard floor. The steam from the kettle filled the kitchen and floated up to the ceiling. "Chrissie, either make the tea, or take the kettle off," Mary said with a sigh.

The noise of hobnailed boots hitting cobblestones could be heard outside. The four members of the Caffery family held their breaths. Maggie quickly bolted the door just in case it was the RIC. Shadows crossed the kitchen window. Then Maggie shouted through fear. "For God's sake, the rossers are not going to use the back door." She unbolted the door and opened it. The two brothers stood in front of her, unharmed, both were in shock with blood splattered over their clothing.

"Mammy, it is them, Christy and Alec." The three women embraced the two men. Mary cried, "My boys, my boys. I knew you would be safe. I prayed to the mother of God to keep you safe. Girls get some water on, these boys need a wash, a drink and something to eat."

Alec replied huskily, "Whiskey would be good Mammy." James smiled totally oblivious but happy that everyone had stopped crying. Alec and Christy were relieved that they did not take James to the game.

Chrissie left the room quietly. She went to the room she once shared with Mammy and Maggie. Tears fell as she looked out the bedroom window and down the street, it was a dirty foggy night. She whispered, "Michael, please remain safe, please come back to me." Downstairs in the kitchen, Maggie looked to the flagstone floor in utter despair. She had no one to turn to or tell, she was isolated in her forbidden love.

Chrissie saw a shadow outside the bedroom door, then heard a gentle tap on the door. It was Alec. "Chrissie, Michael is safe. I saw him, he told me to tell you that he is safe." Chrissie sobbed into her brother's arms, her body shook with the pain. She loved Michael more than life itself.

The two brothers left the football ground with twelve dead and sixty wounded. The British Government in effect condoned the 'Black and Tans' behaviour and their unofficial reprisals. However, this attitude did not go uncondemned in Britain, especially by the press. Even the conservative Daily Express was appalled by the 'Black and Tans.' The average soldier was ashamed of them too. Due to the public outcry, the 'Black and Tans' were sent home in disgrace.

Weeks later, Dick told Maggie he would soon be going home. He held Maggie's hand in his and said, "I will be back. We will have a life in Ireland, in your Ireland, Maggie's Ireland." However, Maggie was confused, the awful events of Croke Park brought danger to her home. In a way she was glad Dick was going and she hoped the feelings of betrayal would go with him on the mail boat back to Wales. Yet, her heart was full with love.

"Dick, I will write to you every day but do not write

to me until I tell the family about you." Then Maggie sobbed, as Dick held her in his arms. He breathed in her hair, felt her soft innocent body next to his. He knew it was time for him to leave, he pulled her closer and whispered the line from the poem, "I will seek you again through the world's end you whom I found so fair." Dick left. Maggie cried like she had never cried before. Her heart was breaking over the uncertainty of their future. Yet Dick knew he would be with Maggie.

The British knew early in 1921 that they could not win, so did the IRA and Sinn Féin. The Anglo-Irish war was not winnable by either side. The Anglo-Irish Treaty was signed on December 6th, 1921 and was passed comfortably by Parliament on December 16th, 1921. However, in Ireland, the reception of the Treaty was a different matter.

January 1921. Dick was no longer a British soldier, he was an apprenticeship painter and decorator with Cardiff Corporation. Maggie continued to write to Dick and he in turn looked forward to the lavender scented letters. One morning, while in work and on his tea break, Dick sat in the empty hallway and wiped paint from his hands with a rag full of turps. He took out Maggie's recent letter, breathed in the lavender, rolled a cigarette, took a sip of tea and read.

Dear Richard,

On my birthday, 13th January, British troops, manning a check point on O'Connell Bridge, opened fire at a crowd of civilians, killing two and seriously wounding five. There are soldiers on the roofs with machine guns. I am terrified and too scared to tell my mother about you. It breaks my heart because I love you so much, but I think it is best that we part. Margaret.

Dick's heart stopped beating. He then reread the letter, rubbed his eyes, then stroked his chin and walked outside towards the gate, leaned on it and then lit a cigarette.

In Dublin at Leinster sewing factory, among the monotonous whirring noise, were rows of women's heads, bent over their singer sewing machines, dust motes hung in the air, a slither of sunlight wafted through the high windows. Maggie, who was always the life and soul of everything, was withdrawn and due to lack of sleep she began to look ill, this created gossip.

Maggie lined the shirt under the needle to attach the cuff, tears fell onto the garment. She stopped and wiped her tears. She could not tell, say or share her heartache. Her friends stared at her in confusion. Ruth touched Maggie on the shoulder and whispered in Maggie's ear. "Are you okay, Mag?" Maggie bit her lip and nodded yes. "Well you do not look it, let's meet up after work, and see what's on at the Lyceum?"

Maggie said, "No, I need to be home."

Dick spoke to his mother late one evening and confessed his love for the young Irish woman. His mother listened while sipping tea. Dick's cigarette smoke swirled around the kitchen, creating a grey mist. He then let out a sigh. Charlotte looked at her son, into his clear blue eyes he had inherited from his father. She noticed there were pools of sadness there. She placed her hand on his and spoke, "Dick, what is your mind telling you, not your heart, but your mind?"

Dick let out a cough and quietly said, "I am in love with her and I want to marry her and live in Dublin."

Charlotte stopped breathing and thought, *Living in Ireland how often would I see him. Florence is in Hereford, Victor's gone to America.* The thought of Dick leaving made her shudder. "Dick, let's get some sleep, a tired mind is not a good mind."

172

The following morning, Dick lay in bed, his younger brother James made snuffling sounds. Dick watched the sun's rays dance through the thin curtains. He had not slept a wink, he tossed and turned. Yet, he knew it was fear holding Maggie back. Dick wanted to bring light and happiness to her young traumatic life.

Downstairs, Charlotte spoke with William, "William, Dick spoke with me last night, he has met an Irish girl, named Maggie." William looked at his wife, and thought on Clara the Irish woman he was married to for two years, and who died in his arms. He thought he would never love again, but he did. He loved every woman that gave him the eye. He thought on his father who he never knew, who was an Irishman, and a sailor from the West Coast. "Lottie, Ireland is not good at the moment, we, the British, are fighting our own, and I think Dick would be better off without this woman, he has a job and is young enough to get over this and find a local girl."

"I think it is too late for that, he is determined."

"He will be better off getting over it and start getting out more with his mates."

Dick stood outside the kitchen door and heard all. He crept back upstairs, packed a few items, left a note for his mother and slipped out into the cold Splott morning.

Dick's mother gently knocked the boys' bedroom door and entered, "James, come on you, will be late for school." She then noticed Dick's bed was empty and a note was left on the pillow.

Dear Mother,
Please do not worry I am travelling to Dublin to see Maggie.
Your loving son,
Richard.

Dick took the overnight mail boat and arrived at Dun Laoghaire on a cold Saturday morning in February, wearing his new grey woollen overcoat and black trilby hat. It began to sleet, creating a swirl of grey white specks on his hat. He caught a cab into Dublin town and, from the taxi window, he could see parts of Dublin were burnt out. He got out of the cab at the bottom of Maggie's street and noticed the skeletal buildings, ink black against the sky. A depressing, foreboding feeling sat in the well of Dick's belly. Yet, in his mind, he kept repeating what he was going to say to Maggie's mother.

He stopped, rolled a cigarette, blew smoke into the air, clouds cleared and a winter sun shone. Dick knew he wanted Maggie to be his wife, the mother of his children. He stopped outside the large gate, where he heard giggling.

Across the street, and unbeknown to Dick, stood Dermot O'Hara, Dermot placed his right hand inside his coat pocket, not to keep his hand warm. No! He felt the cold steel of his gun as he watched the skinny young man in the fashionable coat and hat.

Dick placed his hand on the latch, when suddenly the gate was flung open. He jumped and so did Maggie and Lily. Lily had called on Maggie to chat about old times. Dermot was waiting to walk Lily home. Dick coughed the words, "Hello, Maggie." Lily noticed the accent was not Irish.

Maggie was speechless, she stood with her mouth opened wide. "Dick," she gushed.

Dick replied, "Maggie, I have come to see your mother and ask her permission to marry you."

Lily and Maggie looked at each other in stunned silence. Then Lily saw Dermot. She leaned forward, took Maggie's hand and held it, and then her republican friend whispered, "Maggie, I will call and see you later this evening." The young lovers stared at each other. The passion was still there and this sparked the fire of desire.

A voice from inside the house shouted, "Maggie, why are you standing with the gate and door wide open!?"

Maggie forgot who Lily and Dermot were. She knew

175

this was what she wanted. She wanted to be with the man she loved. Maggie stood on her toes and whispered in his ear, "I can't believe it is you. I thought I would never see you again, and now you are here." She held Dick's hand, shut the door and led him into her home. The heat stung at Dick's cold cheeks, making them bright red and highlighting his beautiful blue eyes. He quickly looked around him and noticed the house was spotless. Mary was in her kitchen ironing her son's clothes, she looked up with flushed cheeks.

Dick looked smart in his winter coat, he always dressed smartly. Dick, painfully thin and only five feet and six inches tall, took off his hat and droplets fell onto the floor. He nervously played with the edge of the trilby while stood in front of the short, stout, very round Mary Caffery and held out his hand. "Hello, Mrs Caffery. I am Richard Griffin, from Cardiff, and I would like to ask your permission to marry Margaret."

Mary shielded her eyes from the sunlight, then Dick's words leaped into her ears. She sat down in her old oak chair, the colour drained from her face. She stared at the young, painfully thin boy with the mop of auburn hair and she thought. *Did he just say he wanted to marry my daughter?* Maggie tearfully spoke, "Mammy, are you all right?"

Mary was shocked and lost for words, then found her

voice, "Am I all right, what sort of question is that, am I all right? Maggie, you are a keeper of secrets, who is this English boy?"

Dick's thoughts were clouded, clouded by naivety and his love for Maggie. He knew the Caffery house was republican. Maggie never disclosed much about her two brothers and never mentioned her brother-in-law was in the IRA. In the deathly silence, Maggie's pent up guilt and fear and the hidden love spilled out in tears and large sobs.

Then Dick's Cardiff accent pierced the air. "Mrs Caffery, if you would please hear me out, I can explain."

James, who was sat in the corner, became agitated. Mary responded angrily. "Margaret, wipe your eyes, you will upset James, you know how sensitive he is." Maggie stopped, wiped her eyes in her cotton hankie, and gave James a weak smile and reassured him that all was well. Mary glared at Dick and said, "I am all ears."

Dick was a man who did not like confrontation, but his love for Maggie helped him to find his voice. "Mrs Caffery, I was conscripted in 1918, I never had a say in the matter.",

Mary made the sign of the cross and said under her breath "A British soldier. May God forgive you Margaret, because I will not!"

177

"Mrs Caffery, I am of Irish descent, my grandfather's family came to Wales from the West of Ireland, fleeing the famine. When they left Ireland they thought they were heading for America and when they sailed up the Bristol Channel they thought it was the Hudson River. After landing at Cardiff it dawned on them they were in Britain."
Dick placed his hat on the table and stopped to roll a cigarette.

Mary stared open-mouthed, Maggie sat with her head in her hands. James smiled at the man with a funny accent. The air inside the house was full of betrayal, guilt and Dick's cigarette smoke. "I love your daughter and would like to marry her."

Mary looked to the flag stoned floor and felt sick with this shocking betrayal. She looked out the window, the baby blue sky had disappeared, replaced by heavy leaden clouds. Anger rose in Mary and she spat out. "Margaret, how long have you been seeing the enemy?!"

"Six months, Mammy," Maggie gulped.

"Are you out to bring shame on this family? Margaret, answer me? I need an answer, has the cat got your tongue?"

Maggie was rooted to the flagstone floor, she could not find the words. Shame had grabbed her tongue, and then her love for Dick released it.

"Oh, Mammy, I love Dick, he is a good man, he is on our side and understands our plight and is willing to live in Ireland with me."

"He wants to live in our country? Get out of this house now, not you, Maggie. Get out of my home, and do not darken my door step ever again. YOU ARE NOT WELCOME HERE!"

Dick was shocked, he had not thought about the consequences. He did now. His bowels jolted and he needed to use a toilet, as he turned to leave, Maggie screamed, "NO!"

Alec, Maggie's brother, stood in the doorway and heard all and he felt the pain of betrayal. The anger was mixed with bile, the bile had turned into acid and stung the back of his throat. Alec coughed, all three turned around, then Alec recognised Dick. He thought the soldier looked too young to be in the army and he noticed how thin he was. But most of all his blue eyes, they were the lightest blue he had ever seen. Alec said in hushed tones. "Mammy, I know this man."

Dick looked bewildered. Maggie's face was red with emotion, Mary could not believe what she was hearing. "I know you, you're the Brit that sometimes turned a blind

179

eye," Alec said quietly. Dick said nothing, his heart was thumping, and he knew there was no going back now. "Well, this is a civilised house, why isn't our guest sat at the table, being waited on?!" Alec barked.

The two women moved swiftly, a kettle was put on the stove and bread was being cut and buttered. Dick and Alec sat at the table and spoke in hushed, nervous tones. Christy came in from the yard and was introduced to Dick and was told the truth about Maggie and the Brit. He too was in shock, his shock was soon replaced by anger. He glared at Dick, his knuckles were white, ready for a fight.

The clock chimed 7 o'clock and at the same time there was a knock on the door. It was Lily Murphy.

Earlier, Lily ran after Dermot and, when she caught up with him she placed her arm in his, like any normal courting couple, and then they began to walk. "Lily, what was all that about?" Dermot whispered in her ear.

Lily replied out the side of her mouth. "I think he is a Brit and after courting one of our own."

"Aye, he is a marked man."

"Dermot, you remember when I told you of the poverty that I lived under, when I was a young girl, and the girl I befriended?" Dermot looked confused, then nodded.

"Maggie accepted me for being me and would take me to her home and there I was treated like I was one of their own. That was her house that I came out from. I know she and her family have republican leanings."

"I hear what yous are saying but he is the enemy, and his girlie, the friend that showed you kindness."

"Please, Dermot, let me handle this."

"Yous will have time. I will give you forty-eight hours and that's that."

The door was opened by Alec. "Good evening, Alec."

"Do I know you?"

"Yes, I am Lily Murphy from the tenements." Alec stood to one side, with his mouth wide open and let Lily enter and thought, *Be Jaysus, what a lovely girlie you turned out to be.* "Evening, Mrs Caffery."

"Ah, Lily, your timing is wonderful, have you come to join the friendly society?"

Lily looked confused, she accepted the chair from Christy who invited her to sit. Lily noticed Maggie had been crying, her eyes were red and puffy. The Brit was sat at the other end of the table, far away from Mrs Caffery. "Please can I have a word with Maggie alone?"

"No!" Mary said sternly.

"Mammy, let them be," said Alec.

Both friends left the kitchen and went out into the courtyard. The cold night air mingled with the hay. "I will not mince my words, Maggie; we know the Brit is a British soldier."

"WAS, and his name is Richard, Richard Griffin."

"All right, was."

"Lily why are you questioning me? You cannot stop me from being with Dick."

"No, Mag, we can't, and it is your choice and decision. You are courting danger with the ex-soldier. Richard Griffin has forty-eight hours to leave Dublin."

"You threatening me, Lily?"

"No, I am being brutally honest with you. See it from an Irish point of view, an IRA point of view."

Maggie called Alec out to the yard. Alec wandered out, hands deep in his pockets.

"Can you tell Lily about Richard?"

Alec noticed Lily's beauty, it took his breath away. He never thought that skinny Lily Murphy, with the nits, would turn into a real lady. He was astounded. He recalled the tenement block where Lily lived and the stench of living cheek by jowl, and sharing the one toilet between sixty poverty stricken families. He felt admiration for this woman for how she rose from the poverty and bettered herself.

Inside the house Dick played with the edge of his hat, Christy and Mary sat and stared at him, yet his love for Maggie kept him anchored to the cold flagstone floor. Dick had never had feelings for anyone until Maggie. He firmly believed he and Maggie would be married. He thought, *Christy and his mammy can stare as much as they like, I am not budging.*

Out in the yard, Alec coughed and sneezed and was about to wipe his mouth in his sleeve when he realised he had a hankie in his pocket and thought, *Manners, where are my manners.* "Lily, is it really you?" Alec blurted out. Maggie elbowed him in the ribs. "Is the crush still there, Lily?" he said out of devilment. They both laughed, not Maggie. "Joking aside, the Brit inside, sorry I meant Dick. I would often see this soldier hang out, why I am telling Lily this?"

"I am engaged to Dermot O'Hara."

A deathly silence hung in the air.

"Jaysus, Lily, how do you do it?" Alec spat out.

"Richard Griffin has got to leave, and leave soon."

Alec spat the words out. "That man, who is sitting in my mother's house, often turned a blind eye when patrolling the dock area. I did not know that he was me sister's friend."

Alec was interrupted by Maggie, "Lily, may I remind

183

you, Dick is no longer a British soldier and he came here this evening for his love for me."

Inside the house, silence hung in the air like smog. It was broken by Dick, who decided to leave the tensed air of the kitchen and Mary's stoney face that said nothing but if looks could kill, he should be dead. Christy followed Dick out into the yard. "How yer all doing?" Christy said.

Alec replied through clenched teeth. "Do you really want to know? Lily here is only the fiancée to Dermot O'Hara."

Christy gulped, Dick went pale and thought, *Bloody hell, what was I thinking?* He looked to Maggie, then realised the reason why he came. He wanted to be with this woman for the rest of his life. The three siblings and Dick looked towards Lily. Lily spoke, "Maggie, Richard must be on the boat within the next forty-eight hours."

Dick's Cardiff accent punctuated the air. "I will go but I still want to marry you Maggie."

Alec, Christy and Lily returned to the kitchen where Mrs Caffery was holding on to the sink. She had heard all and her anger had now turned to fear, fear for her children and mostly for Maggie.

In the yard, Dick put Maggie's small delicate hand to his lips and looked into Maggie's eyes. As he kissed her hand, a tear fell down her cheek. Dick caught it with his pale, white, freckled hand and kissed it and looked longingly into her face and said, "No one, or anything, will come between us, Maggie, we will be together forever." Maggie melted into Dick's eyes. Dick walked away beneath a blanket of stars. Maggie waited for him to turn the corner and then walked across the yard she saw her brothers feeding and grooming the horses for tomorrow's round. With a heavy heart, she went inside the house to face her mother. The kitchen table was spewed with tea cups and buttered bread that was stiff at the edges.

Mary saw the pain in her youngest daughter's face. Yet, she saw love in her daughter's eyes. Mary turned away from Maggie and went into her best room and sat in a chair by the window. She felt a chill go right through her so she pulled her shawl around her shoulders, took out her rosary beads and prayed to the virgin mother for forgiveness, forgiveness for herself and for her child. Mary's anger had now turned to concern, concern for her daughter's safety.

Mary looked around the room, to the oak table that was basic, four unmatched chairs that matched in the dark, to the picture of 'The Blessed Virgin Mary' and her sorrow filled face. Mary saw the way her daughter looked at the Brit, and how he looked at her. Her eyes drifted to the family

185

photos, Christina and Michael's wedding, her children when younger.

Maggie finished clearing away the dishes, she then dried her hands. Christy came in and threw Maggie a black look, Maggie tried to speak. Christy raised his hand and said, "I have nothing to say to you," and walked away. Alec stood in the doorway, letting in the cold air, Maggie shivered, then Alec kicked the door shut. Maggie was close to her younger brothers but, over the last few months, she had become distant.

Alec spoke, "Maggie, sit down, let's talk." Maggie nodded and sat opposite her brother. Alec spoke through gritted teeth, "I cannot believe you, all that we have been through and you fall for a Brit."

"I did not set out to do this. I never had any dealings with British soldiers until Richard."

"Maggie, let's hope word does not get out, because not only will you be ostracised and punished, the whole fecking family will!"

Maggie was shocked to hear her brother swear, she began to tremble, then anger rose inside her. "How dare you speak to me like that! Richard is no longer a soldier, he is a civilian."

"Maggie, keep your voice down, you have already

done enough damage."

Maggie left the kitchen and opened the door to the best room and whispered, "Mammy, are you all right?" Mary jumped from the past to her youngest daughter's future. She entwined her rosary beads around her arthritic fingers, the orange glow from the gas light reflected through the lace curtains onto the white beads and added light to the oppressive, dimly lit room. Mary remembered the pain she went through with Chrissie. She stretched, sighed and heaved herself out of the chair, put her rosary beads away and shut the door.

In front of her stood Maggie, face wet with tears. Mary pulled Maggie to her and both sobbed. They walked into the now empty kitchen, Mary put the kettle on, she turned and saw the anguish in her daughter's blue eyes. Mary remembered how she had behaved towards Chrissie, and she vowed she would never behave that way again. Mary looked to her youngest daughter, "Margaret, it is obvious Richard Griffin is very fond of you for him to travel from Wales to here in these troubled times"

"Mammy, I wrote to Richard to end the relationship and that is why he came. I love him and want to be with him. He is willing to stay and live in Dublin."

"Margaret, let's hope and pray word does not get out,

regarding your relationship with a British soldier, because if it does, it will be best that you leave before anything evil happens." Mary stopped in mid-sentence, her heart was breaking. Maggie was twenty-two and the furthest she had ever been was nine miles up the road to Sandymount.

"Mammy, he is a civilian now."

"Let's go to bed, it has been a long day." Mother and daughter left the warm kitchen and went up the stairs to the cold bedroom where Maggie tossed and turned all night. Maggie woke, her mind was heavily burdened, and she had no appetite for breakfast.

The family prepared for mass. Outside a bitter wind howled off Dublin Bay. The family with their heads bowed made their way to church. Maggie looked up, she saw Chrissie, there was no greeting, both walked in silence. Then Chrissie spoke in hushed tones. "Maggie what have you done? Did you not think of the consequences?"

"He is no longer a soldier."

"But he was!"

Maggie sighed, she'd had no sleep, she felt weary and alone. All her family were against her, except her mother. Both sisters stopped and looked at each other. Then their mother drew near and angrily said, "Go on, the pair of you, attracting attention from others. Chrissie, may I remind you of your courting days with Michael. If I were you I would shut up now and you too, Maggie."

At home Mary laid down the law to the family that Dick could visit and the family had to be civil to him.

That evening Dick strolled in the bitter winter air. Dermot was in the pub over the road and was looking straight at the handsome, red-haired Welsh man. Dick opened the gate to the yard and Maggie was waiting, "Come in Dick, we will go out the back." He took her hand and kissed it, her face flushed bright red and the flames of desire flickered in their very being. He kissed her on the mouth and feelings soared through both, neither had experienced love and lust combined.

They walked into the kitchen, Alec and Christy were there, along with Chrissie. Mary was sat in the corner, Dick stood in front of them and apologised for all the trouble he had caused. A deathly silence hung in the air. Maggie played with the lace on her blouse, Chrissie looked at Dick, Alec looked to his feet. Christy sat and stared at Maggie. Mary stood up and told Dick to take a chair and to sit down. Then Chrissie spoke, "So this is the enemy my little sister's fallen for."

Dick quietly spoke. "I am sorry, I would like to stay here with Maggie and live in Ireland."

"You have no chance," Alec said, while rolling a cigarette.

"I want to marry Maggie, and I know she wants to marry me. I have booked my ticket for tomorrow. I will leave on the mail boat in the morning at six thirty." Maggie gasped and held Dick's hand.

"The sooner the better," said Chrissie.

Maggie icily replied, "Chrissie, remember how I stood by you many times, so please keep your opinions to yourself." Chrissie stared silently at her younger sister. Mary asked Maggie and Dick to follow her into the best room where she lit the oil lamp that was on the windowsill. Dermot O'Hara saw this and he knew it was a sign that Dick was leaving Ireland, he downed his pint and left the area. "I am going to leave the two of you alone. Alec, come in here, I want you to be Maggie's chaperone. When I say alone, I mean with her brother."

Dick looked perplexed and stifled a giggle. Alec walked in and sat between Maggie and Dick. Mary left the room. Then the three let out a nervous laugh. Dick spoke, "Your mother confuses me and frightens me at the same time."

Alec replied, "Ah, she means well, how far is Cardiff from London?"

"London is in England and is over a hundred miles from Cardiff." Dick then turned to Maggie and told her about Catholic church in his street, called St Albans."

Alec replied, "Well, Mag, Mammy will be pleased that there is a Catholic church in Dick's street."

The fumes from the oil lamp mixed with the cigarette smoke lingered in the room. The pretty patterns reflected on the glass globe oil lamp and shadows danced on the room walls. Alec felt uncomfortable and he thought the young couple should be alone. The clock chimed eight o' clock, an hour had passed and it was time for Dick to leave Maggie. Alec left the two at the gate. He walked to the back door and turned his back on the lovers so they could have some privacy in their parting.

The two held onto each other and kissed passionately. Neither wanted to leave. Dick stood back and stared hard, then whispered, "Remember you I found so fair" Then he turned and walked away. Maggie watched through a veil of tears as Dick turned the corner.

Michael appeared out of the blue, Maggie jumped. "That's him, is it Maggie? The man you are giving up your family for and betraying Ireland?" He pointed his gun at

191

Maggie, but did not fire. Maggie felt faint, and fell against the gate.

Chrissie heard her husband's voice. "Michael is that you?"

"Ah, Christina, I have come to look at the man Maggie stabbed Ireland in the back for." Both sisters looked at each other, there were no words left.

"Excuse me, Mrs Morrissey, are you ready for the walk home?" Chrissie smiled but not with her eyes. The married couple walked, arm in arm, home.

Alec silently witnessed all. He felt anger towards Michael, but he also understood Michael's anger. Inside the house, Maggie would not tell her mother about Michael. Her mother had enough to put up with. Mother and daughter looked at each other, there were no words left and both women were emotionally worn out.

In bed that night Maggie tossed. The following morning she struggled to get up for work, she knew life had to go on but she found living unbearable at the moment. She dressed and went downstairs to the warmth of the kitchen, she looked to the clock, it was 6am. She gulped. Dick would be on the mail boat now. She stared out to the yard, Christy looked towards the kitchen window and he nodded his head at her. Alec opened the large gate to let the horse and cart out and gave a stoical smile.

Mary whispered to her daughter, "Maggie, come and drink your tea, the porridge will not be long."

"Mammy, I am not hungry, but I will drink my tea." Her mind was restless, she thought on Ireland, yet her love was stronger for Dick than for her country and this sometimes startled her. Mary glanced at her daughter, turned to the sink and wiped a stray tear.

Maggie met Chrissie, both walked to work together in silence. Then Chrissie turned to her little sister, she noticed how ill Maggie looked. Her heart filled with compassion and she put her arm round her little sister. "Is he worth sacrificing your own country for? Is he Maggie? We might never see you again and think what this is doing to Mammy."

"I love him with all of my heart, and yes I have chosen Dick over Ireland, and I will have to face the consequences, not you." Both sisters hugged each other.

Dick arrived in Cardiff late on Monday. He decided not to catch the tram so he walked down Newport road. This cleared his head but not his heart. He knocked the door, it was quickly answered by a tearful Charlotte. "William, it's Dick." William, James, Doris and Charlotte all waited to greet him.

Dick sat at the table with his parents, holding his head in his hands as his father went on and on about Maggie. Dick slammed his hand on the table, making his mother jump, he glared at his father. "You are in no fit state to preach to me about the woman I love when you have broken my mam's heart many times! I love Margaret Caffery and will marry her at St Alban's Roman Catholic Church whether you like it or not!" Dick kissed his mother goodnight and that night he slept like a baby.

Two months later, on a sunny day in early April, Maggie received a letter from Dick.

Dear Maggie,

I hope you are well and your family too. I have booked our marriage for May 19th at St Alban's Roman Catholic Church. Please send your baptism papers as soon as possible. I have taken out our war bond too. I miss you terribly.
Please give my best regards to your family.
Your ever loving Richard

Maggie held the letter in her hand and ran to her mother who was in the yard putting washing out. "Mammy, I have a letter with my marriage date." She gave the letter to her mother.

"Oh, Maggie, he has lovely hand writing. So it will be a May wedding. A May wedding, that is not a good sign, if you marry in May, you rue the day."

"Oh, mammy, I don't believe in that superstitious nonsense." Mother and daughter laughed.

The letter confirmed Mary's hidden fears, she had hoped the love would wane between Dick and Maggie, she prayed that time and distance would kill the love. She was wrong. The love grew stronger.

Chrissie breezed into the kitchen, spring air caught the hem of Mary's dress, strays of hay scattered, April sunshine spread to where the three women were sat at the kitchen table. Tea was poured, buns were eaten and the day's gossip done. Maggie was happy but slightly apprehensive of how Chrissie would take the news.

Mary looked at her two daughters. She noticed how beautiful they both were. Chrissie's light green eyes, her thick lustrous hair and Maggie with a beautiful smile that would melt any heart. Mary coughed and spoke, "Chrissie, Maggie will be married on May 19th." Chrissie stared at Maggie, her mouth agape in shock. Maggie shielded her eyes from the sun, she only saw shadows of Chrissie and then the sound of the back door slamming shut.

Chrissie's heeled shoes were tapping the yard, her face was hot with rage, her hands clenched. She spoke aloud, "I was wrong, I cannot believe Maggie would leave us and Ireland behind, after all we have been through. God, I am fuming."

Mary placed her hand on her daughter's, Maggie looked to the table, realisation hit her and she mumbled, "No one will be attending my wedding."

Mary spoke, "Maggie, are you sure you want to do this?" Maggie continued to stare at the pine table wishing she could sink into it and disappear. She scraped the crumbs from the buns, took the dishes and stumbled towards the sink dropping a cup that shattered onto the flagstone floor. Maggie kneeled down to pick up the broken crockery, and stayed on her knees for what seemed hours, but in reality it was only minutes. "Maggie, come on child, you cannot stay down there forever."

"Mammy, I am not sure, I need to think, I need time to think." Maggie got up and sat with her mother.

Mary spoke, "Do you love him?"

Maggie nodded yes and then looked her mother in the eye and replied, "I do love him and I want to be with him." She paused and then continued, "I want to stay in Ireland with Dick," and then she broke down, "Mammy, why can't I stay in my own country?"

"Maggie, you made a choice and must remember Dick was once a British soldier."

"Mammy, he was with a peacekeeping force, not a 'Black and Tan."

Irish republican Maurice Moore was executed by the British and a province of Northern Ireland was created. Maggie wanted out, she had had enough. She posted her baptism papers the beginning of May.

It was 6am in the morning and a pale yellow sun rose from a baby blue sky, Maggie stood in the middle of the yard. She walked to the stables, she heard the horses snuffling and whinnying, the brightness of the morning light was still in her eyes, she blinked and waited for the familiar surroundings of the stable to appear. She stroked the horses and told them of her journey.

She walked back into the house and looked around and gently touched the furniture. She picked up the metal framed photograph, the one of her and her two younger brothers, Alec and Christy, stroked the hook on the back of the door where Alec and Christy hung their caps. She stood in the best room where she remembered the laughter, tears, and the tragic death of Essie on that winter day in February,

1919. She caught her image in the mirror, tied her hair and straightened her brooch, brushed hay from her skirt. She walked back to the kitchen. The bells her mother had given her for her wedding day lay on the table. The Irish proverb that was in a wooden frame, a present from her brothers, glinted in the sun. White Irish linen pillow slips that Chrissie left for her.

She reflected back to the day before when she walked to St Stephens Green, she had opened the large gate, stepped out onto Red Cow Lane and remembered the time her and Lily tied the rope round the lamppost and swung on it for hours. Everything seemed crystal clear, the sky and the buildings. The boozy, ancient wood smell from Jameson's distillery hung in the air. She walked over the 'Ha'penny Bridge,' black and silver arches glinted.

She looked at the bridge's reflection in the river Liffey, past Dublin Castle where Maggie threw a stern look. Through the park entrance and where beautiful bird song greeted her. The laughter from her childhood echoed in her mind, she sniffed the air, and the scent from the early spring flowers embraced her senses. Behind her Dublin was waking up. Trees were dressed in their spring colours, a squirrel scurried about, she watched as it ran up the tree trunk. It reminded her of Lily and how the two of them loved to climb

trees and where her two brothers played hide and seek. She
sat in her own quietness, her hands rested on her lap, she
looked at her bare fingers and thought, *in two days' time I
will be wearing a band of gold.*

She thought on her family and friends and her job at
the sewing factory and where last week her boss gave her a
glowing reference. Her country Ireland came to mind.
Sadness seeped up from her gut to her heart, she twisted her
hankie and she spoke aloud, "I am leaving Ireland but Ireland
will always be with me." The morning light spread and
warmed her back as she made her way home. Maggie was so
in love she did not see Dublin, burnt out and broken, she did
not hear the foot steps behind her or the dark shadow of
Michael Morrissey.

"Top of the morning to you, Maggie." Maggie's belly
tightened as she looked at him with disdain and said nothing.
Through gritted teeth he spoke. "Maggie, as long as I am
alive do not think of coming back if you know what's good
for you and that Brit." Michael then pulled out a gun and
pointed it at Maggie's head.

Beads of sweat formed on her brow, the cold steel of
the gun rested on her mid temple, bile from her belly rose
and stung the back of her throat, and she screamed "Go on,
do it! I dare you, go on, you have been waiting to do this for

months! Go on, pull the trigger, do it!"

He put his gun away and called her a traitor and walked away from his sister-in-law. Maggie shook with fear and spat the bile into her hankie. The word traitor went straight to her true core and she trembled.

Later that morning, Maggie and her family walked to St Paul's Church to mass. Mary Caffery told the priest and friends that Maggie was leaving to work in Cardiff, but some knew different. Inside the church the rows of seats were full. Spring flowers were placed at the front of the altar and added colour, the scent of flowers, incense and candle wax filled the air. She followed her mother and brothers in to the pew.

Chrissie came in late and sat next to Maggie and never uttered a word. The mahogany pews creaked and groaned like an old ship. Father Flynn spoke to the flock regarding Maggie and her new life in Cardiff. She will be missed but we wish her well.

After mass, Lily Murphy, Dermot O'Hara and other well-wishers gathered. Dermot held Maggie's hand in his and whispered into her ear, "You made your choice with the Brit, don't think of coming back." She looked up into his eyes and smiled yet inside she was terrified and the word traitor rang in her ears. She felt weak and dizzy and again she questioned whether she could go through with marrying Dick. She looked around her and realised Dublin was burnt out, terror and despair hung in the air. Maggie chose peace and love, she knew in her gut that peace in Ireland was a long way away.

The family went back to their home where a special tea was prepared in honour of Maggie. Songs were sung and family stories were told. Chrissie was the last to leave, she stared at Maggie and walked away. Across the street was Michael, eyeing Maggie and mockingly cocking his gun. Deep down, Michael knew Ireland's freedom was a long way off and for a moment he envied Maggie.

Back in the kitchen, she remembered the time she lit the candle for Christmas and placed it in the window. This ritual could only be done by the youngest girl whose name was Mary. Maggie was the youngest girl and her full name was Margaret Mary. She always felt special in taking part in this Irish Christmas tradition. She and her brothers picked holly for Chrissie and Essie to make a holly ring for the front door. The aroma of baking bread with caraway seed and fruit would waft up the stairs to their bedroom.

On St Stephens's day, a procession would take place where a pole entwined in holly was carried from house to house. She remembered her mother telling her a story when she was younger. How the pole had a dead wren on it, and the image of the dead bird made Maggie cry.

She eyed the seashell that had been on her mother's kitchen windowsill for years, she picked it up, placed it to her ear. She went back to where she ran barefoot on the sand, paddled in the sea, and picked winkles for tea. Maggie sobbed uncontrollably as grains of sand fell onto the kitchen table.

She scraped the sand from the kitchen table into a small pile, walked out into the yard and dug a small amount of earth. She mixed this with the sand, then wrapped it in her hankie, and put it with her gifts. Her mother watched her daughter from the kitchen window and sighed. The boys went out and nodded to Maggie. They had prepared the horse and cart for their sister's journey to Dun Laoghaire, and the mailboat.

James nervously coughed, then gave Maggie a sprig of a shamrock. This kind gesture made her weep. This confused James and he spoke, "Why are you crying, Mag? Don't you want to go on your boat trip?" James's innocence made Maggie smile and she hugged her older brother. A sleepy sun spread its rays, added more light to the yard. Maggie was still in the kitchen, apprehension gurgled in her belly. Her family stood in the yard. Maggie took one last look and breathed in her family's familiar smells. Head down, she gingerly walked to the cart and to her waiting family.

The Caffery family sat on the cart for their seven and a half mile journey to Dun Laoghaire. Alec held the reins, the horses snorted, snuffled and swished their tails in the early spring morning. Maggie looked around and suddenly, she felt fear trickle down her spine. She looked around again, looking for shadows of Michael or Dermot. She looked to her mother, and her mother squeezed her hand. James smiled at her. Maggie forced a smile, her throat constricted. Her two brothers were deep in thought, there were no words left to be said. Silence hung in the air like a cloying mist. She anxiously pulled her carpet bag near. She could smell the Irish Sea, it was beckoning her, embracing and inviting her away from the violence and pain.

At the dockside, Alec left the horse and cart. Maggie and her family said their last goodbyes. A keen wind caught the hem of Maggie's skirt showing her slim ankle. Her mother Mary saw the smoke from the mail boat sway towards Dublin Bay. Maggie hugged her mother, and then shook hands with her brothers, she held onto Alec's hand the longest.

As she walked away from her family, she felt dizzy and her bottom lip quivered. Once on the mail boat she looked towards Carlisle Pier, the pier was where families waved loved ones off. She saw her mother and three brothers leaning on the stone wall. Suddenly she saw Chrissie, Chrissie had defied Michael. She waved her white hankie in the air and shouted, but Maggie was deafened by the noise from the docks, seagulls and her own sobs. She held onto the rail of the ship, breathed deep and found inner strength, she waved to her mother and her siblings until they shrank into five tiny dots.

Part Two

Wales

Out in Dublin Bay, Maggie wiped her eyes and looked up to the heavy leaden sky, rain spat at her face and plopped onto the deck, adding to the misery. She twisted the strap of her carpet bag round her fingers and cried above the nautical sounds. The sea had gone from dark green to steel grey and white horses rode the sea's back. The mail boat shuddered, then pitched and rolled. Alone on the deck, the boat tossed about but she sat in silence. She was wrapped up in her own thoughts, her family, the wedding, leaving Ireland. Maggie had her own inner storm.

The bleakness of North Wales was in the distance, the Island of Anglesey jutted out. It was a damp drizzly day at Holyhead, North Wales, the port was busy, she was lost in the crowd and felt tears prick the back of her eyes. She swallowed hard and then made her way to the train station. The criss-cross glass roof of Holyhead station and the red brick walls and the stench of coal disorientated her.

She breathed deeply and asked for a one-way ticket to Cardiff General. She could not understand the ticket officer's accent, when he told her she must change at Shrewsbury and when he told her she had seven stops before Shrewsbury. The voices around her were not her voices, the people were not hers and this country was not hers. Maggie looked inside the carpet bag to her wedding outfit, she clasped it shut and hugged the bag to her. Maggie wore the suit she had made for Chrissie's wedding, and the very fashionable French hat called the cloche. The hat was grey with a lavender band, this matched her light grey suit and pale lilac blouse However, the smoke from the incoming train brought smut that lingered and created black smudges on her clothing.

The engine hissed to a halt, droves of people got off. The station master shouted, "Train for Shrewsbury." Maggie got up, straightened her skirt and hat. She gingerly got on the train for its four-hour journey to Shrewsbury. She made her way into a six-seater carriage and sat by the window in silence. Four men had joined the carriage, two smoked a pipe, that made Maggie cough. The four conversed in Welsh. This confused her so she turned her attention to the window and watched green fields, hedges and villages whip by. She forgot about the seven stops when she saw the sign for Shrewsbury, the train slowed down, the ticket master shouted, "All change please, all change."

She shakily stepped off the train, straightened her clothing and then found out she had an hour wait for her connection to Cardiff. She was thirsty and hungry, then she saw a sign for a tea shop. Maggie opened the door and a bell tingled, the aroma of the tea shop was so inviting and the tables were neatly made with small vases of pink carnations and stark white lace doilies. She saw a pleasant looking woman behind the counter. "Oh, hello, please can I have a cup of tea please and a…" Maggie stopped in mid sentence.

She was interrupted by the Englishwoman, who rudely told Maggie, "You are Irish, I refuse to serve you."

Maggie looked confused, she tried to speak but was prevented and was asked to leave the tea shop. She walked outside and looked up to the glass veranda roof, saw a flock of starlings and thought, *What have I done? I am so stupid. If the Irish hate the Brits, the Brits must hate the Irish.* She was no longer hungry or thirsty, her belly was full of fear.

The train for Cardiff arrived and this train had a buffet car, but Maggie didn't know anything about the buffet car. The smell of food from the buffet car guided Maggie to its whereabouts and in a quiet voice, disguising her accent, she ordered tea and a bowl of soup with a roll. She sat down to eat, she glanced out the window and watched the border of England and Wales flash by. The tomato soup tasted delicious, after eating she dozed.

The train whistle woke Maggie, through blurry eyes she saw the sign for Cardiff and the large clock that said 6.30 pm. She rubbed her eyes and stretched her stiff body.

Sleepily, she humped her carpet bag off the train. She held her hat in her hand and her travel bags in the other, her hair had come loose from its bun. She sat on the cream and brown Great Western Bench, her trembling hands smoothed down her creased skirt. She felt grubby and unclean, and a great sadness washed over her. The clock chimed 7 o'clock and there was no sign of Dick. Her tired thoughts went back to Carlisle Pier and to the five dots that were her family and her world. She gingerly made her way to the ladies room.

Back home in Ireland, Alec, Christy and Chrissie had gone to their place of work. Mary sat in the kitchen and stared blankly out the kitchen window towards the yard. James rocked back and forth, "Mammy, we have tea now?" Mary did not stir, she continued to stare towards the Celtic sea to Wales and her daughter Maggie. "Mammy we have tea?" Mary sighed, would she ever hear Maggie's voice again or the word Mammy from her youngest daughter.

"All right, James, I will put the kettle on, you butter some bread, child."

Dick was late, he had missed the tram from Splott. He ran up Newport Road, heard the train, his heart raced when the whistle blew. He had been waiting for this moment for months. He took off his overcoat, threw it over his arm and continued to run. He looked a right dandy in his new tweed suit, and shirt with the gold looking collar studs, his tie matched his pale blue eyes. He paid the guard a penny and skipped most of the station steps, breathlessly, he stood on the empty platform.

Maggie heard a tin, tin noise, unaware it was the sound of segs from Dick's shoes hitting the concrete and sounding like a horse in full gallop. She opened the door from the ladies' room, she saw the back of Dick's head, she would have recognised that thick head of auburn hair anywhere, she shouted his name. Dick turned around, his face flushed from his run.

The lovers both ran to each other. Dick picked Maggie up and then he pulled her down, so he could kiss her. They embraced each other, then Maggie gushed. "Oh, Dick, I thought you might have forgotten about me, the crossing was terrible, a woman in England ordered me out of her café because I am Irish…"

Dick consoled her. "Maggie, I am here now and no one will ever hurt you, ever." Dick kissed Maggie's face. He took her bags, Maggie tidied her hair and put her fashionable hat back on, put her arm in his and the two lovers strolled out of the coal-smelling station and onto Penarth Road where they took a tram. Dick paid the fare, Maggie looked out the window and saw the large Victorian houses standing stately, with white gables and wonderfully colourful painted doors. The tram stopped to let passengers off.

She saw a large sign on a guest house window. She rubbed her eyes and looked again in disbelief, she turned to Dick and pointed to the sign. **'NO BLACKS. NO DOGS. NO IRISH.'** Maggie's face paled, she nudged Dick. He put his arm around her and sighed, "I will never let anyone hurt you."

Railway Street consisted of rows of terraced houses and, where the front doors opened on to the street, Maggie noticed the area was rundown and saw children playing in bare feet. Dick knocked the door to his parent's house. Maggie's belly churned, the door was opened by petite Charlotte, her hair gone grey, tied in a bun and she spoke, "Welcome to Wales, Margaret," and opened her arms to greet her future daughter-in-law. Maggie hugged Charlotte, at the same time she looked to the floor, noticed the oil cloth was bare in parts, then the smell of freshly baked cake, wafting through, inviting Maggie in.

Behind Charlotte stood a short, handsome man, with red hair streaked with white and dancing blue eyes. He put his hand out to Maggie. "Hello, Margaret, I am William, Richard's father, welcome to our house."

Maggie heard giggling and Dick's two sisters poked

their heads from behind the kitchen door. They both had strawberry blonde hair. Doris was a young girl of seventeen, she worked in the local drapery shop. Charlotte had just turned eleven and was still in school. Victor, Dick's brother, had finished his two-year boilermaker apprenticeship and decided there was nothing in Cardiff for him so he had emigrated to America. James was out playing. Florence had moved to Hereford, and was married to William Hill.

"Thank you, Mr. Griffin," said Maggie in a quiet voice.

"Do you know my first wife was Irish? She died young."

"Oh, I am sorry."

"No need to be sorry, Lottie is a wonderful wife and mother." Maggie noticed how much Dick looked like his father. William carried on talking,"Our next door neighbours, the Smiths, are Irish. Michael has lived next door for fifteen years, lovely people."

Charlotte encouraged her shy daughters. "Come and say hello to Margaret."

Maggie interrupted, "Please, call me Maggie."

"Come and meet Maggie, Doris and Charlotte." They shyly came to Maggie.

Doris spoke first, "It is lovely to meet you Margaret,

sorry Maggie, are you excited about tomorrow?"

"I am, but at the moment, I feel a bit sad."

Charlotte smiled, but not with her eyes, and, in hushed tones, she spoke, "Maggie, come into the kitchen, you must be hungry. I have cooked a lovely lamb stew and baked Bara Brith." Charlotte noticed the girl was on the verge of tears, she took Maggie's hand and they all walked into the kitchen. Maggie dabbed her eyes with her hankie and the earth and sand she gathered in Dublin that very morning cascaded onto the kitchen floor. Maggie stared as her tears dripped and mingled with the sand and earth.

Charlotte ordered everyone out of the kitchen, even Dick. She gently held Maggie's hand, "Maggie, it has been a long day, you are very tired and emotional. A big upheaval, leaving your family behind."

Maggie sniffed, and told Charlotte about the sign she saw while on the tram, and the way the Englishwoman spoke to her at Shrewsbury. "I cannot believe us Irish are hated so much."

Charlotte reassured Maggie she was safe in Splott. "We have a very strong Irish community here in Splott. Wipe your eyes, my child, you have your lovely wedding to look forward to." Charlotte's grey hair glinted in the downing sun's rays, she had a very kind open face. Maggie noticed that when Charlotte smiled she had a gap in her front teeth, and this gave her face a young appearance. Maggie let out a sigh and Charlotte spoke, "Maggie, we have tidied the front parlour for you and Richard, it is your home until you find a place of your own." Charlotte saw the anguish on Maggie's face, stroked her hand and said, "Richard loves you." Maggie nodded and dried her tired eyes. The two women embraced, Charlotte then called her family back into the kitchen and they all sat round the table.

The red chenille table cloth had seen better days, the kitchen was basic and plain but, unbeknown to Maggie, William was not a good provider, Charlotte had to make do. Dick looked towards Maggie and winked, Maggie gave a weak smile.

After the delicious tasty meal, Charlotte and her two daughters collected and washed the dishes. This chore reminded Maggie of home, she offered to help, but she was told she was the guest. The heat from the kitchen flushed Maggie's cheeks, suddenly she felt very tired. She asked Charlotte could she go to her room.

"Of course, sorry, Maggie, you haven't even unpacked yet. Come with me, *Cariad.*"

"What is *Cariad*?"

"Cariad means love in Welsh."

The door opened, revealing a small drab room, yet on the floor were rag rugs made from many colourful pieces of material which added brightness to the room. The bed was opposite the window, beside the bed was a small table covered with a white table cloth. On top was a brass lamp, the stand was cast iron and engraved into the glass globe were delicate flowers. The brass was so shiny you could see your own reflection. The oil lamp, reminded her of her mother's lamp back home in Ireland. Maggie stroked the table and she wondered would she ever see her mother again. Either side of the window were two very old armchairs that were full of wood-worm. She blew out the oil lamp, walked over to the window and drew the threadbare curtains. An orange glow threaded through from the outside gas lamp and this lulled her to a peaceful sleep.

The following day, May 19th, the Griffin house was full of laughter. Dick was not at home, he had left the night before and was staying at his grandfather's home at Adeline Street. Florence arrived from Hereford with her husband William Hill. William was Dick's best man. Florence had the thickest head of hair Maggie had ever seen, it was deep red and Florence's face was full of friendly freckles, with a wonderful smile just like Dick's. Florence and Maggie became happily acquainted. Dick's three sisters followed Maggie into her room. Charlotte had left the house earlier.

Maggie's wedding outfit was draped over the arm of the chair, a pale blue skirt and matching jacket, white blouse with lace attached to the front of the blouse and cuffs. The outfit she made herself and it fitted her shape so neatly. The girls sat on the bed, chatting and watching. Maggie picked up a comb entwined with pearls, she placed the comb on her lap, she then brushed her long chestnut brown hair that flowed down her back and past her waist. She twisted her hair and entwined it round her fingers, using pins to keep it in place, she then placed the comb in her bun. The pearl white beads lit up her face and from the reflection in the mirror the three saw her smile. Her three future sister-in-laws gasped, "Maggie, you look lovely." She walked over, slipped her tiny feet into slub silk, off-white shoes and stood up.
"I know this is my wedding day, but I feel so sad."

The three sisters looked shocked. Then Florence spoke. "Maggie, it must be hard, but I remember when I left home and moved to Hereford, it took me a while to get used to the accents and their countryside ways. Dick loves you and I know Mam and my siblings will take care of you." Maggie smiled and asked to be left alone for a moment.

The young bride to be looked out the window onto the working class street and its terraced houses that all looked the same. The sun raised its head and shone on the roof tops, flocks of jackdaws and crows caw cawed. Maggie picked up the bells her mother gave her, she held them close and breathed the gift, hoping to smell her mother. She remembered her mother's words. "It is an Irish wedding gift, representing peace and harmony in the home." She looked at the family photos she brought with her. Her heart was heavy, and her belly gurgled with nerves, she whispered, "Come on Maggie Caffery, you can do this, this man is your life now."

A gentle tap made her jump. Charlotte walked in with a fresh posy of spring flowers and gave them to her future daughter-in-law. Maggie's face beamed, she took the posy and put the flowers to her nose and breathed in their freshness. The posy consisted of butter cups, wild yellow pansies, daisies and dog violets, all entwined in green ivy. Charlotte spoke, " I entwined the ivy to remind you of Ireland." Charlotte stopped and held Maggie's hands in hers and gulped. Her pale grey eyes looked into Maggie's eyes of deep blue. "Maggie, may I say, you look beautiful and I know that you and Richard will be happy."

Charlotte wore a drab looking blouse, yet the posy of blue 'forget-me-nots' pinned to her blouse added colour, the black skirt had a sheen on it, from the many times it had been ironed. Her hair had been put up in a bun and she wore a pale lilac bonnet. Maggie saw a pair of old lace gloves in Charlotte's worn-out dry skinned hands. Charlotte smiled and said, "Maggie, it is tradition that you have something old, something blue and something borrowed. The blue is in the posy, the old is my lace gloves that I wore on my wedding day and the borrowed, my silk hankie."

"Thank you so much. I have some shamrock that my brother James gave me before I left…" Maggie stopped in mid-sentence and swallowed hard and she thought, "I will not shed any tears on my wedding day."

Charlotte held Maggie's hand and the two women walked towards the front door. William stood with his three daughters. Young Charlotte wore a pale lilac, chiffon dress, Florence and Doris wore suits with matching pale lilac blouses. William wore a dark suit, the only suit he owned. The door opened and the spring air greeted the wedding party. Dick, James, his brother-in-law, William Hill, and Granddad Evans had gone on ahead.

It was a mild morning with a few grey white clouds on a pale blue sky. Maggie put her arm in William's, the three women and little Charlotte followed behind. Charlotte hated to draw attention, William drew enough on his own he had an eye for the women and Charlotte was fully aware of this. Some neighbours came out and cheered and sent good luck wishes. The Gothic looking building of St Alban-on-the-Moors Catholic Church came into view. The church was built in 1911. Dick joked to Maggie and said the church was specially built for her because they knew she would be coming. Maggie stood outside with William, the remaining Griffin family and their relatives had gone inside the church. William turned to Maggie, "Maggie, you look lovely, I wish you and Richard a very happy life together."

Maggie thanked William, but her smile belied what she really thought. She felt so alone, utterly alone. This was meant to be her big moment, her day and not one member of her family were there to witness this happy occasion. She reflected back to Patrick, her father, the stories he told her and her siblings, the way he sang while harnessing his horses. Then she thought on her mammy, and a lump of grief lodged in Maggie's throat. Suddenly there was a loud bang and Maggie jumped and felt panic, fear was at her throat, she clutched the posy to her. She looked about her and thought on Michael Morrissey and Dermot O'Hara. William let out a laugh, "No need to be alarmed, it is only a train shunting."

She swallowed the acid bile of terror and walked into the stone cold church where the clip of her heeled shoes

echoed off the walls. Dick looked over his shoulder and saw Maggie. Maggie looked up and smiled, the smile that Dick fell in love with on that cold September day in Dublin.
She saw the priest and the small congregation sitting in the pews. At the altar was Dick, the man she gave her country and family up for. William Hill, his best man, was beside him, William and Florence were the main witnesses to their marriage.

At the aisle Dick squeezed Maggie's hand and whispered thank you. Maggie smiled and her spirit rose. Happiness beamed out from her being, and she knew this was where her life was now.

Their wedding reception was back at the house, a table full of food and a separate table for the beer, sherry and glasses, and lots of laughter and singing. Dick's face was flushed from his couple of bottles of ale, Maggie was tipsy from her one small glass of sherry, the happy couple were leaving to catch the five o'clock tram into Cardiff. They were staying the night at the Angel Hotel. Family and friends waved them off. As they rounded the corner onto Newport Road, Maggie and Dick could still hear the happy boisterous voices.

The tram arrived. Maggie sat at the back of the tram, she ignored the racist signs as the tram made its way to

Westgate Street, the centre of town. They got off the tram at the corner of Westgate Street, Dick turned to Maggie and said, "Mag, this was where the river Taff once flowed, they changed the river's flow to make way for the general train station." Maggie smiled and nodded. Both crossed over the busy road to the grand entrance of the Angel Hotel.

Dick held the door open for Maggie, as she walked in she looked up in wonderment at the large crystal chandelier, the bright glass light lit up the reception area. Their feet sank into the plush, claret red carpet, both made their way to the mahogany reception desk. "Good evening, please, can I help you?" said a tall elegant woman wearing a crisp, whiter than white blouse.

"Yes, we have a room booked under the name of Mr and Mrs Griffin," Dick said confidently.

"Ah, yes, you were married today?" The married couple both nodded. "Congratulations to you both."

The elegant hand tapped a bell and within seconds a porter appeared from nowhere, a small stout man with a thin moustache and thinning hair. The receptionist smiled and said, "Mr O'Grady will take care of you, please enjoy your stay."

"Good evening and congratulations," said the porter.

The porter's accent startled Maggie. He took Maggie

and Dick's one bag up to their room and the newly-weds followed. The three walked in silence along the carpeted hallway past many gilt-edged large paintings and mirrors.

The porter opened the door to a large room into which you could have fitted the whole downstairs of Dick's house. From the west facing window you could see the Castle wall. There was a large bed with a dusky pink bed spread and, in the corner, a pink velvet chase lounge, a marble floral sink, two chairs and a dressing table. Gold lamps were either side of the bed.

The porter bowed and Dick thanked him and gave him a tip. As the porter made his leave, Maggie plucked up the courage and asked the porter what part of Ireland he was from. He replied, Tipperary and asked Maggie where she was from and she replied Dublin. The porter then said in a reassuring way, "It's a good country, Wales, I have been here ten years." Maggie smiled and thanked the porter again.

She went over to the heavy laced window and pulled the lace to one side and looked out to the busy street below. She looked across to the wall of Cardiff Castle and noticed the different animals that were sculptured on the top of the wall. Lions, leopards and wolves. The sun reflected its shadow onto the castle wall and to where the Bute family still lived. Dick put his arms around Maggie and smelt her hair. "I love you, Maggie Griffin." Maggie put her arm around her husband. Dick spoke, "During the war, the US Navy took over this splendid hotel and named it the Chattanooga."

Maggie laughed and, with a giggle, said, "I do enjoy your history lessons."

He pulled his wife to him and they kissed passionately. Then he spread his arms and said. "Well, Mag, what do you think I said I would make our wedding night a night to remember?"

"A beautiful room and my handsome husband what more can I ask for."

The following morning, they were woken by tapping on the door, and a voice on the other side of the door, saying, "Room service." Maggie pulled the bed covers up to her eyes while Dick got out of bed in his Long Johns. He opened the door meekly, took the tray from the young chambermaid, and shut the door quickly.

Maggie laughed at the sight of her husband in his Long Johns, holding an elegant tray. Dick had forgotten he had ordered room service. "Good morning, Mrs Griffin, breakfast is served."Dick placed the gold tray with a white, bone china tea set that was edged in gold, and a rack of sliced toast with boiled eggs in china egg cups.

Maggie with a sigh replied "Ah, Mr Griffin, I could get used to this life you know."

After breakfast they made their way down the elegant stairs to the reception area. They paid the bill and thanked the staff for their hospitality. The Sunday morning air gave them a friendly greeting. They crossed the deserted street and walked through Bute Park, and on to Sofia Gardens. The beautiful gardens reminded Maggie of Phoenix Park. They strolled through, the trees had sprouted newborn leaves, the grass looked fresh and new. They sat on a bench and watched the river Taff go by. Dick spotted a heron. "For its size, it is so graceful." Maggie nodded. Dick held her hand in his. "Are you well, Mrs. Griffin?"

"I am grand, just grand."

"Would you like to see our lovely Civic Centre?" Maggie nodded yes.

They walked through the tree lined path and where various bird song filled the spring air. They stopped and watched a couple of squirrels scurry about, then crossed over the bridge that spanned the Glamorgan Canal, on to the elegant Civic Centre. Dick pointed to a large elegant building. "See, Mag, that's Cardiff City Hall, my father had the contract to paint the walls and ceilings."

"It is very pretty, but Dublin seems so much bigger," Maggie said with a sigh.

Dick suddenly blurted out. "Do you have any regrets?"

"In my heart, I am happy with you, but my mind keeps thinking of me family, sat at home. All the troubles going on around them, and there's me having a stroll with me new husband."

"Let's take the tram to Roath Park, and I will show you where I played when I was a child."

The tram stopped outside the park gate, both walked hand in hand to the boat house and lake where the water lapped and boats were waiting to be rowed. "Come on, Mag, let's have a boat ride?" Dick paid the young man, and helped Maggie into the wooden boat with its two seats and oars sticking out. Maggie tried to enter the boat elegantly and nearly fell into the lake. They both giggled like two children.

He steered them away from the boat hire station. Once out in the middle of the lake Dick looked about him and noticed that they were alone on the lake. He cleared his throat, laid the oars across the boat and sang. The folk song 'Maggie.' "When I first said I love only you Maggie..." Maggie looked up to the cloudless sky and smiled.

Back in Dublin, Mary, James, Chrissie, Alec and Christy were sat at the kitchen table with only sadness for company. They were surrounded by the violence of Irish men turning on their own. Brother fought brother. The family said a prayer for Maggie, and her new life in Wales. James asked when Maggie was coming home. Mary left the kitchen, walked out into the yard and looked up to the sky and said a prayer. "Hail, Mary, full of grace..." She stopped and spoke out loud, "I know I will never see my youngest daughter again. I feel it in my very being but please take care of her, she is so young." Then Mary sobbed into her hankie.

Six days after Maggie and Dick's wedding, the IRA suffered their biggest single loss. Eamon de Valera, the leader of Sinn Féin, gave orders for Michael Collins to stage an operation to destroy Dublin Custom House. The building was the seat of Irish local government and administration. Its destruction paralysed unpopular activities, such as income tax collections. However, it was a military disaster. The IRA were nearly destroyed, six volunteers were killed, twelve wounded and some seventy of the best of the Dublin Brigade were arrested. Their ammunition was low, some of the volunteers had only four or five rounds left.

The Prime Minister, Lloyd George, met in secret with

Eamon de Valera in a London office. Months later, Lloyd George laid down a threat to Sinn Féin. If they did not come to London to discuss peace there would be war within three days. De Valera, a renowned and skilled chief negotiator, refused to meet with Lloyd George, Churchill and others. De Valera wanted the soldier, Minister of Finance, the organiser of the IRA, the man behind the Flying Squad, the man Britain hated, yet, had no idea what he looked like.

The man with a £10,000 price tag on his head, Michael Collins! Collins told De Valera "I am a soldier, not a politician. I do not want my cover blown." De Valera ordered Collins and Griffiths to go to London. On December 6th, 1921, Griffiths, Collins and other colleagues reluctantly agreed to sign the Anglo-Irish Treaty. Michael Collins insisted, and quite rightly, that he had signed his own death warrant.

Ironically, Lloyd George was bluffing. They did not have the resources and British public opinion was profoundly against a return to the Anglo-Irish War. Britain's reputation regarding the Black and Tans was badly tarnished.
Michael Morrissey now fought his own brother Liam. Liam was pro-treaty and supported Michael Collins, Michael backed de Valera. While Britain sat on its divide and rule policy again! Maggie's family were traumatised by civil war.

Maiming and slaying was taking place down the road from where they lived, around the corner and in their backyard.

Britain kept the North kith and kin. Ireland was cut in two. The sore festered, the Catholics in the North felt they had been betrayed, left to be crushed under the RUC and British rule. Eight months later on 22nd August, the Commander-in-Chief of the Irish National Forces travelled to Cork. He was warned not to go but he replied, "They will not shoot me in my own county." He was wrong!

Within a year Maggie had given birth to a baby boy named William Patrick. William was named after his grandfather William and after Maggie's father Patrick. William was known as Paddy. In March 1923, Maggie gave birth to a beautiful baby girl named Charlotte after her mother-in-law. The family of two moved out of Dick's family home, to rooms off Railway Street.

One evening, while their two children were sleeping Dick and Maggie were sharing an evening meal. "Maggie, I have heard in work today that the Corporation are building new houses in a place called Ely."

"Oh, Dick, I pray that one of those houses will have our name on it."

Maggie and Dick now had three children, another boy named Richard who was known as Ritchie. The two rooms they rented were very cramped and Maggie always felt uncomfortable using the communal kitchen and bathroom. She prayed even harder.

One late afternoon, Dick arrived home from work tired, but still he managed to play with his three children. Maggie came in with a cup of tea and a letter. Dick looked up and said "A letter from your family, Mag?" Maggie's smile disappeared from her face and she felt slightly sad. Dick saw this, he put his daughter down in between her two brothers and went to his wife. "What is it, Mag?" Maggie then realised this was the best news they had ever had and she beamed and smiled the smile Dick fell in love with.

Then Maggie cried, "Cardiff Corporation have allocated us a property at Pethybridge Road, Ely. A brand new three-bedroom house, a new school nearby called St Francis with a church hall next door. My prayers have been answered, Dick." Both danced and hugged each other as Paddy, young Charlotte, and baby Ritchie looked on.

Sadness was round the corner. In 1927, Dick's mother, Charlotte, died at the age of forty seven. Charlotte had become a replacement mother and assisted in the births of

Maggie's three children. Deep into the night, Dick and Maggie shed silent tears. "Dick, your mam made me the woman I am today, she gave me the strength to carry on and I will never forget that."

"Yes, Mam was a quiet woman with inner strength, she knew she was loved by her children. Do not worry about Dada, he will not be lonely for long."

The family of five left Splott in a removal truck. The five sat in the truck with their worldly belongings. Maggie stared out the truck window in wonderment, she had never been any further than town. The truck drove on to the busy Cowbridge road, past Ely Paper Mill, the brewery and racecourse. The hops filled the air. Then up the tree-lined Grand Avenue past elegant bus stops and shops. Many new houses with greens in between.

The Griffin family stood outside their new home. At the same time many other families were moving into their new homes too. Their new home had electricity. Maggie and Dick kept flicking the light switch on and off in wonderment. The children's laughter bounced off the new painted walls and bare floor boards. Behind the house were allotments. Dick put his name down and soon learned to grow a variety of vegetables. The Griffin family had fresh vegetables and some fresh fruit throughout the year. Maggie, a trained seamstress, made all her children's clothes. By the end of the 1920s, three more children, Kevin, Alexander known as Alec and Veronica were born.

Maggie and Dick sat at their kitchen table shelling peas and broad beans. "These strikes are frightening, so glad you work for the Corporation, Dick."

"Well, Mag, the way I look at it is, we had the best coal, steel, iron and ship building in the world but no, we went to war and lost a lot of money. I'm afraid we did not modernise these important commodities. The rest of the world did. Now our working class are going hungry."

"Dick, it reminds me of the Lockout in 1913, when me and Chrissie came out on strike." Maggie stopped and tried to imagine the family back home in Dublin. "Dick, I wrote to the family with our new address and still no letters. This makes me sad. Yet, I tell myself off and realise how blessed we are. We have a lovely new home, you have your job. I sew and you grow vegetables and we have six beautiful children."

Dick winked at his wife and said, "Maybe more children, Mag." Suddenly, a small chubby hand appeared, grabbed a handful of peas and gobbled the lot. Maggie said with a laugh in her voice, "Alec, you little villain." Then

Maggie and Dick laughed till their ribs ached.

During the depression of the 1920s and 30s, Maggie turned to the church and her faith gave her strength and her love for her children kept her mind and heart stable. Maggie and Dick were truly in love and this created a good marriage and a happy family.

Letters

On a cold February day in 1933, Dick was in work, Paddy, Charlotte and little Ritchie were in school. Maggie received a letter from Ireland, she had not heard from her family since 1922, though she often wrote to them, they never wrote back. Maggie placed the letter with post mark Eire, inside her pinny pocket and fed her three remaining children, later while the three took their nap, Maggie made herself a pot of tea, sat at the kitchen table and opened the letter, suddenly Maggie gasped and dropped the letter and placed her head in her hands and sobbed.

Dear Maggie,
I know it has been a long time but we thought you should know. Mammy died on the 13th February...

Memories came flooding back, she swiftly went from sadness to anger and in a panic she fled the warmth of the kitchen, ran outside into the arctic weather to the top of the garden, fell to her knees and wept. She composed herself when she heard baby Veronica crying. She wiped her tears in her pinny and swiftly returned to her role as mother.

233

Weeks later, a memorial mass was held at St Francis's Church Hall that was adjacent to St Francis's school. Maggie said her own goodbye to her mother with her children by her side.

Not long after she had another daughter named Sheila, Sheila was dark-haired and her complexion was old Irish, just like her grandfather Patrick.

In the summer of 1935, Maggie, heavily pregnant with her eighth child, received another letter from Ireland. Alec wrote to tell her James passed away peacefully on 30th July. Maggie felt sad, but she no longer cried for her Irish family, she had a large family of her own. However, from time to time Maggie would ask the priest for a memorial mass and she often took her children to remember their Irish family. Another son was born, Francis, followed by two more children, Kathleen and David. Maggie instilled responsibility into her four eldest children to look out for their younger siblings.

Alexander, known as Alec would mitch off school, just like his mam. Then one day, Maggie received a letter from the school concerning Alec. Maggie went up the school to complain and to tell the headteacher that she took Alec to school herself that very morning. The headmistress agreed with her but then went on to say, "Mrs Griffin, when your back is turned, he leaves the school before you do."

Maggie just stared at her feet with embarrassment. "I am sorry, Miss Clarke, he will feel the back of me hand when I see him."

One day Francis was in class and was instructed by his teacher that at 3pm he must go to the headteacher's office. All day he was restless, he thought. *Had someone snitched on him for playing pitch and toss?* 3pm arrived and he stood outside the oak door with a brooding look and a troubled mind. He was not scared of the teachers but was terrified of his mam and bringing shame on the family.

The headmistress, Miss Clarke, boomed "Come in, Young Griffin." Francis gulped and thought. *She's got good eyesight, she can see through doors.* Inside the room he stared past the headteacher's ginger-haired bob and to the picture of the Virgin Mary, looking Nordic and saintly, wearing pale blue and white. "I have a letter for your mam, you must take it home, and do not think of opening the letter, because I have eyes everywhere." Francis gulped and thought, *Yeah, I know and you can see through doors.*

By the time Francis arrived home he was a bath of sweat. He slowly walked through the kitchen, boiled cabbage hung in the air, his mam was standing by the sink. Francis gulped, "Mam, I have letter for you." He handed the letter over and put his shaking hands back in his trouser pocket. He watched as his mother opened the cream envelope and waited with bated breath to see if his mam raised her right hand and formed a fist. "Ah, Francis, me good-looking son with a singing voice of an angel. They want you to sing at Miss Gallagher's funeral." Francis nearly fainted but then he smiled his beautiful smile.

A week previous, the teacher, Miss Gallagher, was run over by a car outside the school gates and died at the scene. Francis sang 'Beautiful Dreamer' at the teacher's funeral. The headteacher, Miss Clarke, whispered to Francis's new teacher, Miss Cunningham, "Voice of an angel, but a devil for the pitch and toss."

Second World War

In 1939, Britain declared war on Germany after Germany invaded Poland. In 1940, Paddy, their eldest child, joined the Royal Welsh. History was repeating itself in the Griffin family. While Paddy was in London waiting for embarkation, he met his future wife Evelyn. Evelyn McNally came from Dublin. Evelyn was 'in service' in London. When Paddy brought Evelyn home to meet the family, seven-year-old Francis said he had never seen anyone so beautiful.

Ritchie, aged sixteen, ran away to sea. Maggie was so distraught her hair had gone from chestnut brown to steel grey over night. She cried to her husband. "My God, Dick, what if they find out our boys are Irish." Dick looked confused and rubbed his eyes in disbelief. "Maggie, our boys are Welsh, they were born in Wales." He held his wife close, he knew the fear of reprisals never left Maggie.

Ritchie was with the Norwegian Merchant Fleet from 1939 to 1945. His ship was called the *M/T Garonne*. From 1943 to 1944, The *Garonne* had its first female radio operator. The *Garonne* was part of a convoy of ships. Ritchie and the crew often sailed in treacherous waters. The last couple of years of the war they had aircraft protection. These very brave men kept Britain fed.

In 2014, Ritchie and other merchant seamen finally had recognition for their part in the food convoys and were presented with medals for their bravery.

During the war years, Cardiff reminded Maggie of Dublin, bombs anti-aircraft guns, carnage and blackouts. Dark memories began to invade Maggie's thoughts, only Dick knew and he could not be there all the time to reassure her. The family would race to the Anderson shelter where Francis, Kevin, Alec and little David thought it was a great adventure but to their mam it reminded her of Dublin during the troubles 'Ireland's war for Independence.' Heartburn and worry plagued her and gave her sleepless nights. Francis and his siblings peeped beneath the blackout curtains and looked towards Leckwith woods and would see the sky above the docks ablaze like a red inferno.

Often, St Francis School would be closed early. Francis and his siblings thought this was great. But not so great when, one time in class, the children's and the teacher's breath had turned to freezing fog. The boiler had broken down again and the temperature in the freezing classroom had not risen above 40 Fahrenheit and because of this the school closed again.

Francis was often taken to the 'Anderson' air raid shelter along with other children, where they sat listening to the centre of Cardiff being bombed. During the war there was an outbreak of scabies but this never touched Maggie's younger children, she washed them with carbolic soap every evening. They all wore hand-me-downs, yet, were all clean and loved and that was all that mattered to Maggie.

In October, 1943, German bombers followed the railway line from Cardiff's Queen Street, to Whitchurch, Rhiwbina and into the heart of the city and for eighty-three minutes they dropped bombs. The crews from the anti-aircraft guns were away attending a competition. This bombing raid terrified the people of Cardiff and gingerly the city and the suburbs tried to get back to normal life.

In 1944, on 20th March was Cardiff's last red alert! There had been 585 red alerts since June 1940.

In May, 1945 the war ended and the streets came out and celebrated, Paddy and Ritchie returned home safely. On July 5th, schools were closed for the day to allow for voting booths and, within two weeks, Churchill and the Tories were out and in came for the first time ever a Labour government, led by Clement Attlee, and with this came the NHS.

In 1946, Paddy married Evelyn McNally, third generation to marry an Irish woman. Charlotte married Dougie Oakley, Maggie made her eldest daughter's wedding dress. She turned a silk parachute into a beautiful flowing dress. Ritchie married Irene Stuart. In the 1950s Kevin married Joan Parker, Veronica married John Sweeney, Alec married Joyce Wilson, Sheila married John O'Brian and Kathleen married Edward Alm.

In 1954, Maggie finished banking up the coal fire when the rattling sound of the letter box disturbed her. She peeped out from the living room doorway and saw a letter on the mat. She picked up the letter and saw the Irish Republic stamp. She decided to wait for Dick to come home from work. Francis was away doing National Service, David was in work. Dick arrived home and Maggie told him about the letter. "Mag, why are you nervous? I can't believe you waited all day for me to come home. Put the kettle on, let's have a cuppa."

Dick untied his boots and placed them by the back door. Both sat opposite each other. Dick opened his baccie tin and took out one of his own rolled cigarettes and lit it. Maggie began to pour the tea "Mag, leave the tea, I will see to it, open your letter." Maggie wiped her hands in her pinny

then cleaned her glasses and then put them on. She picked up
the plain white envelope using a butter knife to open the
envelope, and then unfolded the letter.

Dear Maggie,
I hope you and your family are well.
I am sorry I have bad news. Michael, my beloved husband of
thirty-four years, passed away...

Maggie sighed, "It's from Chrissie, himself is dead. All these
years I lived in fear. See Dick, there is safe and there is
feeling safe. Now for the first time since 1921, I feel safe."

Dick stood up and said, "Come here, you." They both
hugged each other.

In 1957, the Griffin house was a quiet house, eight children
married, some with children. Only Francis and David living
at home. One Saturday afternoon in early summer, Francis
was sat at the kitchen table listening to the wireless. Francis
was a good looking twenty-one-year-old and he was off work
recovering from a broken leg. He broke his leg while playing
football and the breakage ended his career as a professional
footballer. In his hand was a 'Littlewoods' football coupon
and he was waiting for the results to come in. Maggie was

ironing, Dick was at the allotment.

Suddenly, Francis jumped up and shouted that he had won. In fright Maggie nearly burnt her hand. She looked to her son, then spat on the iron and chastised him for gambling. Francis was nearly on the ceiling with excitement, he told his mother again about the win but she was having none of it. Francis kissed his mother on the cheek. Maggie tried to look angry but Francis was her favourite son so she gently brushed his shoulder and smiled. He grinned from ear to ear and left to see his fiancée, Valerie, to share his news.

Out in the warm summer air, Francis tried to walk fast but the twinge from the healing leg reminded him he still had to take it easy. In the distance was his younger brother, David, coming home from work. Francis shouted across the Grand Avenue. "David, I won something on the pools!" "Really, Frank, well done, drinks on you up the Dusty tonight." Francis laughed.

The following Monday, Francis returned to work at Phillips Electric shop down Cardiff Docks. Francis was still unaware of how much he had won. He had an idea it was a large amount. It was the middle of the week and after work, Francis opened the back door. His parents were sat at the table surrounded by their remaining nine children. Maggie picked up the large envelope and waved it in the air. Francis smiled his beautiful smile and his light green eyes lit up. "Is that letter for me, Mam?" Maggie nodded. He picked up the envelope then put it in his pocket, winked at his family and said, "I will open that later."

Veronica shouted "No, you will open it now, yer little monkey."

Francis replied, "That had you all, didn't it." He took the cheque out, held it to the kitchen window, stared at the figure, rubbed his eyes and said to his mother, "Read that Mam."

Maggie turned to Dick and her children, "Oh, my God! Francis has only won £3,000."

Later, Francis gave £100 each to all his siblings. Maggie and Dick only took their share if Francis gave some of the winnings to St Francis Church which he did, and he married his fiancée a month later.

Maggie goes home to Ireland

Late September, after thirty-six years, Maggie was going home with Dick by her side, and with them, their eldest daughter, Charlotte, her husband Dougie and their three children, Margaret, Christy and Kathleen. Along with the well-off newly weds, Francis and Valerie.

They took the train from Cardiff Central to Pembroke Dock and the ferry to Dublin. An hour into the journey, Charlotte's children were all seasick. Francis and his new bride sat away from the others, they were too in love for anyone's company. Maggie and Dick sat holding hands. Maggie relayed her journey of May, 1921. Dick squeezed her hand, kissed her cheek and said, "We have come a long way since then, Mag."

As Ireland came into view, Maggie swallowed a sob. Then Carlisle Pier. Maggie thought of the five members of her family, her mother, James, Alec, little Christy and Chrissie running along the pier. Her mother and James no longer here. The ferry steered into Dun Laoghaire. Sea birds filled the air along with dock sounds. As they waited to disembark, there was a commotion at the dock side. Francis saw a police officer hitting a begging child and he approached the police officer. Maggie turned to Dick and whispered. "I have not been home in years and he is going to get us all kicked out." Francis and the police officer stared at each other as the begging child fled.

The family gathered their belongings and continued walking through when two men stepped forward. "Hello, Maggie." It was Alec and by his side was Christy. Maggie was visibly shocked, the last time she saw her two brothers they were young teenagers. Her little brothers were grown men now with children of their own. They noticed their sister was thicker round the waist, her chestnut brown hair was steel grey and her glasses looked like jam jar bottoms. Her heart leapt with joy and tears streamed down her face. Then the three embraced each other. Maggie let the tears of the lost years fall on to Alec's shoulder making a damp patch, Maggie apologised. Alec softly replied, "No need to say sorry." Through blurry eyes, brother and sister eyed each other.

Alec and Christy were still carters and their horse and cart were waiting to take them back to Red Cow Lane. Maggie nervously looked at Dick, he held her hand and gave her a reassuring squeeze. Maggie looked to her husband and smiled. Dick was the only one who knew the heartache Maggie went through by leaving Ireland.

The families were loaded onto the two carts.

Charlotte and her family went with Christy. Maggie and the others went with Alec. Off they trotted through the centre of Dublin and on to Red Cow, Lane. Christy and his wife, Maisie, and their three children now lived at Red Cow Lane. Alec opened the large gate to let the carts through. Christy's wife, Maisie, was waiting with her children.

The look and smell of the yard brought back many memories of the dark days, the death of Essie, mostly her mother. She wiped another tear. Maisie, small-boned and with an open face waited to greet her sister-in-law. "Welcome home, Maggie." This touched Maggie and made her cry again. The two sisters-in-law hugged each other. Maggie noticed a change to her family home, there was a bathroom and the exterior looked more modern. Laughter floated in the air, food was eaten. Maggie was exhausted, emotionally and mentally, she dozed off to the dulcet tones of her family.

Later the men and Valerie went over to the pub for a drink. Valerie was possessive and would not let Francis out of her sight, she thought he would run off with an Irish colleen. Over the pub there was lots of singing. Dick encouraged Francis to sing. Francis lifted his head and sang the ballad of 'Kevin Barry' and other rebel songs. His two uncles were surprised that their nephew knew so many Irish rebel songs. Christy's eldest son, Chris, stood in the door way openmouthed. He was so impressed by the way his cousin Francis dressed, looked and sang. He thought Francis was Elvis, the real Elvis! Then Francis sang 'Danny Boy.' You could not hear a pin drop and not a dry eye in the pub. Valerie glared at her husband and at the others, who were admiring her husband's talent. In Valerie's mind, only she could love him.

That night Maggie did not sleep well, ghosts of the past came shadowing her thoughts, Michael Morrissey but most of all her mother and eldest brother James. She gingerly got out of bed not to disturb Dick, she padded down the stairs, opened the back door and stepped into the yard. The autumn air nipped at her face, the sky was a blanket of stars. The horses were stirred by her presence, this reminded her of her father, Patrick. The others were staying in a B &B. Christy and Maisie gave up their bed for her and Dick and were sleeping in the lounge. Maggie felt a presence, it was Christy. "Oh, sorry, Christy, did I disturb you?"

"No, Mag, I was restless myself."

"The past came calling."

"Ah, see, Mag, this house holds many memories for you."

Suddenly, Maggie blurted out the words she had been wanting to say since she arrived in Dublin. "Why did you all stop writing?"

"Mag, let's go into the kitchen and have a warm drink."

Both sat at the table with a mug of tea. Christy coughed, then relayed to his sister past events. "Mag, we were traumatised. It was a good job you got out and I will be honest many times I envied you and your life in Wales. Even Michael turned against his own brother. There was killing, maiming, slaying. You could not trust anyone. I also think 'The Troubles' disturbed Mammy and Chrissie, disturbed their minds. Chrissie became more devout, more than Mammy."

Maggie wiped her eyes and thought. *How could I be so selfish and just think of myself.* "Christy, I am so sorry, I heard the news on the radio and the odd paper but…" Maggie stopped in mid sentence. Maisie entered the kitchen.

"You two catching up and walking down Memory Lane?"

"Something like that," replied Christy.
Maggie had her answer, a painful, raw answer.

The following day after breakfast, Maggie, Dick and their

family prepared for their journey to Bray. Before they left, Maggie and Maisie made arrangements to meet up at Bray and to end the week with a picnic at Phoenix Park. Christy and Alex took the family to Connolly train station and their journey to Bray. Bray was twelve miles from Dublin and was an old Victorian Town.

Maggie looked up to the criss-cross glass roof, the station was hot and stuffy and diesel hung in the air, voices and engine noise echoed throughout the busy station. Maggie's thoughts went back to the conversation she had had with her younger brother. Then apprehension rose from her belly. Her meeting, with her eldest sister, was a couple of hours away.

All clambered onto the train. Maggie took a window seat, the others sat near. Kathleen, Margaret and Christy were excited by the train journey, it was better than the boat trip. Sandymount, Dalkey, and Shankill flew past. The train hugged the coast, Maggie liked that. The children whooped when the train went through the tunnels, showing sea scenes and then the rocky landscape of the Wicklow Mountains.

Finally, the train stopped at their destination. Francis, with his winnings, had rented a large house on the sea front. After a short walk the families arrived at the sea-facing house, that had four bedrooms and two bathrooms. Maggie,

Dick, Valerie, Francis, Charlotte and Dougie had their own bedroom, the children shared the last bedroom.

The men went off for a pint to the local pub while the women unpacked and Valerie helped three excited children prepare for the beach. There was lots of giggling and laughter. Suddenly the front door was opened and a voice shouted, "Hello, anyone home?"

Maggie thought she was hearing things until Charlotte replied, "Mam, someone is down stairs." Maggie stood on the landing and looked down, it was Chrissy with her daughter Maureen. Both grandmothers were grey with age and slightly larger round the waist. Chrissie noticed that Maggie was wearing thick lensed glasses. The two sisters hugged each other. Charlotte and Valerie looked on, then the three children barged in and bumped into Chrissie's daughter, Maureen.

Maureen was dark like her uncle Alec and her grandfather Patrick. Maureen had her two children with her, ten-year-old Billy and thirteen-year-old Bernie. Chrissie was still beautiful, a pair of sunglasses perched on top of her thick salt and pepper hair, giving her an air of sophistication. Maggie introduced her daughter. Chrissie noticed Charlotte had a beautiful open face with chestnut brown hair like her sister's and she thought she saw a glimpse of Essie in

Charlotte's face.

Maggie's daughter-in-law, Valerie, reminded her of Doris Day, blonde and petite. Maggie's three grandchildren, all white-blonde, smiled at the stranger. While other family members were talking, both sisters stepped outside. Chrissie turned to Maggie and spoke. "It has been a long time, Maggie."

"Yes, Chrissie, too long and whose fault was it, Michael's,? he was the main reason I could not return home."

"Leave it in the past, Maggie"

"I cannot leave Mammy and James in the past!"

Chrissie looked to her feet, she felt tears prick the back of her eyes. Michael was the love of her life and she missed him so much. She thought time might heal but when she saw her sister's eyes, full of hate for the man she loved, she knew time did not heal.

Maggie's thoughts went to the conversation she had with Christy and she felt a tinge of remorse. Maggie also knew how much Chrissie loved Michael. "I am sorry for your loss, Chrissie. I know you loved him very much."

"Yes, I did and I miss him terribly too."
Chrissie saw three men walking towards them. She knew one was Richard Griffin, his thick auburn hair had thinned over time, but his eyes were still the same.

"Hello, Christina, surprised to see you so soon."

"Hello, Richard, yes I came early, I wanted desperately to see Maggie."

"Thirty-six years is a long time, please call me Dick. This is our eighth child, Francis, his wife is Valerie and this is my son-in-law, Dougie."

Francis shyly smiled and Christina was taken aback. Francis wore her pale green eyes, she noticed the autumn sun showed hints of auburn in Francis's hair. She was then introduced to Dougie, with his dark looks and a cigarette behind his ear.

Chrissie returned home to her bungalow with her daughter and grandchildren. She had invited Maggie and her family to her home for a buffet meal that evening.

At 6 pm, the six adults and the three children came and stood outside Chrissie's bungalow. The bungalow was small with a bright red door in the middle and windows either side. Charlotte admonished her children in a nice way to behave. Dick opened the small white gate. In the middle of the garden stood a hydrangea. Its pink colour was changing to an autumn blush. Chrissie opened the door and, with a smile, invited the family in. The family walked through the wooden-floored hallway, all wiped their feet on the matted mat. Maureen guided them into the lounge, the centre point was a cream-tiled fire place with a mirror above, a pale grey three-piece suite, photos on the side board and a large photo of Michael Morrissey in full IRA uniform. Maggie looked up and felt slightly dizzy. They went in to the square kitchen with its black and white plastic tiled floor, in the middle of the room was a green formica table with four chairs. Chrissie and her daughter prepared sandwiches, cake and ice cream for the children and bottled beers for the men. Valerie was impressed by the bungalow, it gave her ideas for her new home. Francis was impressed by Michael Morrissey.

The next couple of days were spent sitting by the sea with the children. Francis and Valerie swam with the children. Maggie and Chrissie tried to reconcile their relationship. Chrissie wanted to forget the past but Maggie found it hard. Chrissie's grand-daughter, Bernie, had a small camera and wanted to take family photos. The family gathered with the sun behind them, laughter and seagulls sprinkled the air. Maggie sat far away from Chrissie and looked into the distance. Chrissie tilted her head and smiled.

The following day Maggie, Dick and their family, along with Chrissie, her daughter Maureen and her two children were

travelling by train to Dublin. They were meeting up with
Maisie and her children for a big family picnic at Phoenix
Park. The sun shone brightly as the families walked through
the gates of the Park. The rays reflected autumn colours in
the trees. The young children ran ahead laughing and
giggling. Dick squeezed Maggie's hand and whispered in her
ear.,"Bring back any happy memories?"

"Some, maybe, when I was a young girl mitching off
school."

"I don't believe you, Maggie," Dick said with a smile.

"You know you're still not a bad looking fella." Dick
blushed at Maggie's remark.

Maisie and her children were already in the park. A
blanket was spread and laden with food and drinks.
Children's laughter and Welsh and Irish accents mingled in
with the bird song. Chrissie and Maggie's eyes met, both
women smiled at each other for the first time since Maggie
arrived. Bernie pulled out her camera and caught the image
of both sisters smiling at each other.

Maggie by nature was kind-hearted and, like Chrissie, she
became very devout. She used the power of prayer to take
away the bitter pain of her being forced out of her beloved
Ireland. She realised her life in Wales was more gentle than
in Ireland and, in a way, she had had a lucky escape. Maggie

quipped, "The place has not changed much."

Chrissie laughed and said, "Except for the monument to Gough, it was blown up in July."

Maggie smiled and looked at the surrounding beauty of her favourite park, then to her eldest daughter, Charlotte, and her grandchildren. She saw Francis and Valerie walking hand in hand towards the lake and Maggie thought on her future grandchildren. Maggie smiled then sighed. Chrissie spoke, "A penny for your thoughts, Mag?"

"You always asked me that back in the old days." Both sisters laughed then they stood up. Chrissie opened her arms and both sisters embraced each other.

The night before leaving Ireland, the house was in darkness and all were asleep, except Maggie and Dick. Both were sat up in bed, chatting. "Mag, are you glad you came back?"

"Yes, I am and I am also glad Chrissie and I made up. In the early years, we had both been through a lot and we both found forbidden love in our journey of strikes, poverty and violence. We both made dangerous sacrifices, but at the end of the day, we both made the right choices." She winked at Dick and kissed his cheek.

"Mag, I will never forget those early days in Wales when you often cried yourself to sleep. One day full of guilt, the next day joy, and another day you missed your family so much. It broke my heart to see you in so much anguish."

"Ah, Dick. I lost one family, I was not going to lose this one. Besides, Wales is my home now, where our children and grandchildren were born and I can sing the Welsh National Anthem better than you." She gently pushed her husband. Dick looked into Maggie's eyes, and despite her being fifty-eight, his look still made her blush and go weak at the knees.

50th Wedding Anniversary

In 1971, Maggie and Dick moved from their three-bedroom house that they had lived in for forty-three years, to a new one-bedroom council flat with central heating. The central heating fascinated Maggie, she thought it was a great wonder and would often say, "Ah, the heat from the pipes and no coal." Sometimes, the air was dry and she would put bowls of water next to the radiator. Maggie was also diagnosed with diabetes and her eyesight was failing.

Early morning, May 19th 1971, Maggie felt the heat from the morning sun's rays, the rays created an orange glow that filled the small bedroom that she and Dick shared. Both lay in bed holding hands, when Dick turned to Maggie, kissed her forehead and whispered, "Happy 50th Wedding Anniversary, Maggie."

Maggie smiled and replied, "The same to you, Dick."

That evening Maggie put on a royal blue satin dress and a white lace cardigan, then a white silk hat with a silver hat pin, on her feet were white wide-fitting sandals. Dick wore a suit, white shirt and a plain blue tie to match his wife's dress. Dick held her hand and breathed in the lavender. Then a familiar voice from the passage way spoke, "Mama, Dada, are you ready for your big party?" It was Paddy, their eldest son. Paddy was with his wife, Evelyn, and in Evelyn's hand was a white rose and a spray of white rose with gypsophila for Maggie. Both were surprised. Evelyn helped to pin the spray to Maggie's cardigan, Dick pinned his own. Paddy and Evelyn guided Maggie and Dick to Paddy's Ford Zodiac car. Evelyn opened the back passenger door for her in-laws. Freckled-faced Stephen greeted his grandparents. Paddy's other children, Kevin and Richie, were married and were making their own way to the party.

All comfortably in, Paddy drove down the tree-lined Grand Avenue, where many trees were in bud. Past St Francis RC school, which all their children and most of their grandchildren had attended, past the Protestant school Windsor Clive and many houses. In the middle of the Avenue were the wedding gown colours of the early spring cherry blossom, its petals sprinkled the green like confetti.

Opposite this delightful sight, Paddy turned left into the grounds of The Church of the Resurrection, known locally as the 'Rez'. Trees loomed from a great height and added an air of gloom round the Gothic Church and the surrounding area.

The three generations of the Griffin family got out of the car, Paddy opened the door wide and held his mother's hand. Dick got out the other side. A setting sun adding colours to the sky, rings of gold in between the clouds, all on a pale lilac sky. Paddy opened the church hall door and held it for his parents. Inside the well-lit church hall were tables laden with food and, in the middle, was a white square cake with Happy 50th Anniversary written on it. A small hatch at the back of the hall was a bar.

In the middle stood Charlotte, now a widow, her youngest son, Dougie, by her side. Her eldest daughter, Margaret, now married with children of her own. Kathleen, a pretty teenager, next to her was her brother Christy. Richie, Maggie and Dick's third child worked as a Continental bus driver and was in Europe. His wife, Irene, (Biddy) stood next to their daughter Pamela. Pam stood with her husband and holding their baby. Their son Stuart was to the right with his new wife. Veronica stood with her children Maria, Jimmy, Theresa, Angie, Bernie and John. Johnny Sweeney, her husband, red-faced and looking bemused. Alec was next to his wife Joyce, Marilyn their eldest child just turned eighteen was holding her baby, Paul. Michael, dark like his Mam but with his father's looks, stared ahead.

Julie wore the Griffin smile. Kevin was next to Joan with their children Lorraine, Brian, Keith, Sandra and Beverly. Valerie and Francis were at the back. Malcolm stood next to his cousin, Stephen, Suzie was next to Lynda. Julie, their eldest girl, white blonde hair in a ponytail and wearing red hot pants like her two little sisters, was at the front, her hands on her little brother Sean's shoulders. Sheila was with her husband, Johnny O'Brien, and their two quiet children, Christine and Sharon. David, six feet tall, stood with his wife Pam. Karen, dark haired, Anthony, curly dark hair, Paul, blond and Suzie, jet-black hair. Glamorous Kathleen stood between Eddy, her husband, and Laurie, their lodger. Her two children, Vincent and baby-faced Gina, were in the front.

Paddy, Evelyn and their two sons, Kevin and Richard, joined the Griffin family. Mr. O'Connor, Headteacher of St Francis School, was there along with Canon Cahill from St Francis Church and their long time friends. Maggie and Dick stood laughing and then the Griffin family gathered, surrounding Maggie and Dick with love.

Epilogue

I remember walking up the Grand Avenue with my mother, Valerie. Mam wore a blue dress, my father Francis wore the only suit he owned, I and my siblings trailing behind. My two sisters, Suzie and Lynda and I wore red hot pants, they wore a white blouse underneath. I wore a white, thin cotton jumper and on my feet were bright-red sling back sandals with a small heel. I could not take my eyes off the shoes. Aged ten and a half and these were my first big girl shoes and they were not second-hand!

Malcolm, my eldest brother, wore trousers with a paisley patterned cotton shirt and tie. Sean wore brown shorts and a brown and yellow t-shirt. As we entered the hall, my father warned us to behave, but I was distracted by my shoes. Then I realised we were in the Protestant church hall and I hoped my headteacher, Mr O'Connor, did not find out I was here.

The week before, I was called into his office. I was not a naughty child, so I knew it was not serious. I thought I was going to be milk monitor or the day's bell ringer. He called me in and said, "A little bird has told me that you were going to the Baptist Sunday School." I was amazed a bird had spoke to him. I was a good child and always told the truth and I nodded yes. *"You know you are not allowed to attend this Protestant church hall?"* I gulped and was a bit disappointed because I was not going to be bell ringer or milk monitor. I coughed then looked at the headteacher's large 'Adam's apple' that reminded me of a meatball. I kept staring at the Adams apple. His voice boomed *"Young Griffin, you are not to attend Sunday School at the Baptist church hall because they are Protestants."*

I found my voice and stammered, *"Th, the, they, they are my friends, not Protestants."*

"Off you go and do not let me find out you attended the Baptist Church. You only attend St Clare's on a Sunday and while in school you attend St Francis."

I stood outside the Protestant large church hall and prayed Mr O'Connor never finds out. We followed our parents into the hall to the sounds of much laughter and voices. Then I saw him talking to my auntie. He was in the Protestant church hall. I rubbed my eyes in disbelief. He boomed, *"Hello, young Griffin."* I side-glanced him and stammered, *"Hel, hel, hello, Mr O'Connor."*

The hall soon became packed, making it hot, then someone left a side door open, creating a welcoming breeze. Suddenly Nana and Grampy appeared and the love from me and my aunties, uncles, cousins swelled towards this loving, *beautiful couple.*

After much eating and sliding on the wooden shiny floor. Uncle Paddy tapped a glass for us all to be quiet, he then cleared his throat and sang the Solomon King song, 'She Wears My Ring', we all sang the chorus.

That evening I recall a tall man entering the hall. He was holding a camera and he was not a Griffin. He was a photographer for the South Wales Echo. The family gathered around my grandparents. I stood at the front, a tall girl for my age, trying to hide the gap where my two teeth were, with my hands placed on my little brother Sean's shoulders. The camera flashed and we all smiled.

At the end of the evening we kissed Nana and Grampy and the many aunties and uncles goodbye. It was wonderful to walk home in the dark with our tipsy, happy parents, us babbling children underneath a blanket of stars and a bone-white moon. A night I will remember for ever!

I cannot recall my grandmother saying a bad word about anyone, she had a wicked sense of humour and always saw the funny side of life and she often giggled like a school girl. The last years of their lives they lived in Ely, a suburb of Cardiff, in a one-bedroom council flat that backed on to the

Western Cemetery. She would slap her thighs and laugh and say, "When I die they only have to throw me over the wall." If my grandfather tried to speak she would chastise him in a tongue and cheek way, "Ah, shut up, Dick, no one is talking to you."

Her hands smoothed the floral pinny, the same pinny that wiped many eyes and cleaned inside a few ears, carried many household items and served a great purpose. We never caught anything from her apron, only love.

My grandmother always carried a lace handkerchief and she wore silver hat pins in her various hats. She was a devout Catholic and attended mass religiously, if she could not attend mass, the priest came to her home. She loved the Irish folk group, The Dubliners, and had all their LPs. Ronnie Drew and The Dubliners gave my grandmother Dublin back in song.

I recall one Christmas, my father, Malcolm and I walked up the Grand Avenue in the biting cold, A three-mile walk to Nana's. In my hands, and held close to me, was a winter berry plant called a 'Jerusalem Cherry Plant'. We entered Green Farm Close and I was bone cold but the image of my Nan's face when she saw the plant kept me warm. We did not knock, we walked into the already crowded

room, full of aunties, uncles and cousins. I waited for Nana
to see me. "Ah, and who is this?"

I replied "Julie, Nana."

"Ah, do not tell which Julie, let me feel your face. It's
Francis's Julie."

I shyly smiled and gave Nana the plant. She took it
from me and I followed her into the kitchen. Nana placed the
plant with five others on the window sill. I stared in disbelief
and was crestfallen and then she turned to me and saw tears.
"Ah, to be sure, I have my own orange grove!" I beamed
from ear to ear. She then gave Malcolm and me a tin of
toffees with a sheepdog on the front. At Christmas Nana gave
all her grandchildren, who were under the age of sixteen, a
tin of toffees in a colourful tin. Nana had thirty five
grandchildren!

When her grandchildren reached the age of sixteen, we were
invited to visited our grandparents and were given a five
pound note. Nana eventually lost her eyesight through
diabetes but she turned this into something positive. She had
talking tape books and once a week she attended the Blind
Institute, Newport Road, Cardiff. The very road where she
saw the sign in 1921, **No dogs, No blacks, No Irish!**

Nana recovered from a heart attack in early December, 1977. I remember visiting her with my father, she told me she saw the image of 'The Blessed Virgin Lady' at the bottom of her bed. Nana was devout and an honest, fair woman. I had no reason not to disbelieve her.

June,1977, I left school. I got in my father's builder van and we drove off to Nana's. After tea was drunk and biscuits eaten, Nana turned to me and said, "A little bird told me that Julie has a job in a sewing factory." I nodded yes. She then said, "Ah, like me, I worked in a sewing factory, sewing men's shirts in Dublin." My face beamed that I was like Nana. I was too embarrassed to tell Nana that I turned down a job with Jacobs Biscuits factory in Fairwater, Cardiff, because men wolf-whistled at me when I walked on to the factory floor.

February 1978, Nana died and for the first time in fifty-seven years, Dick was alone. I recall coming home from work and the curtains were drawn. I asked my mother why, and she replied Nana Griffin died today. I was shocked and asked where was Dada, my mother pointed to the long passageway. My father was in the bottom bathroom. I could hear him weeping, Dada never cried. I asked, would he open the door,

he said no, he wanted to be left alone. I understood this,
because Nana was my father's rock and now he had no one to
turn to.

  (Nine months later my father died, aged forty-three.
Nana called her favourite son home.) The funeral mass was
for adults, no children were allowed and at the burial were
men only. Alec, Nana's surviving sibling came over from
Dublin. (Chrissie and Christy had died in 1974.) For the first
time in fifty-seven years, Dick was alone and without the love
of his life.

In 1984, Grampy was living with Veronica and Johnny
Sweeney. Grampy had a fall and was on the floor a while and
because of this he had hypothermia. Veronica had an annex
made for her father. I visited Grampy, who was dressed
smartly, but the light of Maggie was no longer there. We
made small talk. He then asked me would I take his black and
white woollen jacket to work and sew the sleeve.

Days later, at work, I placed the jacket under the needle
when a photo fell out, a black and white photo of a young
couple. When I returned the jacket, I took out the photo and
said Gramp, this photo fell out of the inside pocket. He
looked at me and grinned, then spoke, "Do you not know

who it is?" I shook my head. He coughed, lit a rolled cigarette and said, "That's Nana and me on our wedding day."

A year later, Dick left this world. He let his spirit soar, found his soul mate and they became entwined again.

'Forbidden Love' is part of a trilogy. The second book is titled, 'Gambling with the Family'. This is an extract from the second book.

Gambling with the family

He loped down the street in his over sized boots that knocked against his ankles and toes and made glug, thud sound as they hit the pavement. Through the streets of Ely, Cardiff, down Pethybridge Road, along the Grand Avenue, past the 'proddy' school, turned left at Wilson Road and through the open gates of St Francis Roman Catholic School.

The school yard was quiet but now echoed to the noise of his overlarge boots. He stopped when he saw the capped head of the caretaker Mr. Smith. He waited for him to go into his little den cum office. Francis breathed slower but his palms sweated, he wanted to win again like yesterday. He rolled his penny in his hand, flicked the copper coin towards the wall. It shone like gold in the early morning sun.

His light eyes that were crusted with sleep were now washed clean by the cold air. He wiped his nose in the sleeve of his 'hand me down' jumper that once belonged to his three older brothers. Francis was a bright boy, always top of the class, he had a beautiful singing voice and only a couple of months previously he sang at his teacher's funeral. His teacher Miss Gallagher was run over by a car outside the school gates and died at the scene. He was a natural sports person and was very popular in school.

The game of 'pitch and toss,' gave him a warm feeling inside his belly, he liked competing and when all eyes were on him when he won. He would win again but this was short lived, losing did not sit well with him, the desire to win was now in his veins. Later he ventured into card games, like three card brag and this sustained him for a while.

He left school and started work at Philips electrical shop down the Dock area of Cardiff. The shop sold electrical appliances and records. He would catch the tram into town and walked the rest of the way to Bute Street. Sometimes on the way home he would stop outside the 'Packet' pub and play 'pitch and toss,' with some of the punters.

He was a handsome man with thick, mousey hair with hints of auburn, sea green eyes and a sharp, smart dresser. When Francis walked down the street people stopped and admired, others wanted to chat and share his vibrant personality, people liked being with him. He was also a good footballer and a football scout from Preston North End had spotted him. Francis was on his way to turning professional.

At the end of 1953, Francis was called up for National

Service. Lucky for him the war with Korea was over and peace resumed. He was stationed at Aldershot and there he remained during his conscription. He worked as a clerk and was also courting a pretty dark haired girl named Mary. Mary was the image of the American singer Connie Francis. Within six months Mary broke his heart. The card games at the barracks were a distraction and took the pain of losing Mary away. In 1955 he was conscripted out of the army just before the Suez crisis.

He came home to Rock n Roll. Rock n roll came from America and with this the 'teenager' was born. The youth did not dress like their parents any more they wanted to be like the American singers, Elvis, Gene Vincent, Debbie Reynolds and Doris Day. Francis became a "Teddy boy" Long coat, drainpipe trousers, crepe shoes (beetle crushers) thick hair styled into a DA and in the summer of 1956 there were many dance halls in Ely that played Rock n Roll music.

Acknowledgements

Welsh and their History Gwyn A. Williams.

Great Britain and the Irish Question Paul Adelman and Robert Pearce.

Roath, Splott and Adamstown Compiled by Jeff Childs.

Dublin Tenement Life an oral history by Kevin C, Kearns.

Christopher, son of Christy and Maisie, for O'Donovan Rossa, the layout of 1, Red Cow Lane and the Elvis story.

Joseph Knox, Grandson of Christina and Michael, for the 'family tree' and other stories.

Veronica Sweeney for the photograph of Maggie and Dick.

'Ireland' by Tim Pat Coogan.

'Sapper Martin' by Jack Martin and edited by Richard Van Emden.

This book commemorates the 100th Anniversary of Dick and Maggie's wedding.

It is dedicated to all those who have also suffered for choosing Forbidden Love.

Printed in Great Britain
by Amazon